Looking on Dar

Weary with toil, I haste me to my bed,
The dear repose for limbs with travel tired;
But then begins a journey in my head,
To work my mind, when body's work's expired:
For then my thoughts, from far where I abide,
Intend a zealous pilgrimage to thee,
And keep my drooping eyelids open wide,
Looking on darkness which the blind do see:

Shakespeare Sonnet 27

Chapter 1

Here I am. I don't know how. This place is strange dark and cold. I can see a glimmer of light above my head but no images. I am not uncomfortable I can't feel much at all just the cold. I think I am lying down but I can't get up. I can't move anything but yes I can, my eyes and my fingers maybe. Every part of my body is stuck. Am I strapped down? I can't feel any restraints. Perhaps I am drugged.

Why? I feel a little panic rising; the worm must not come again? I must relax and think. My name is Harriet... Harriet.....Harriet......? Don't worry that will come back. Think! Who am I? Not important, where I am I don't know. I must be alive mustn't I? I try to speak but nothing comes. I smell the air nothing; just cold and damp. I listen; ah... there is something a sound? No a vibration low and regular. Count 1 2 3 4 slow beating like a heart. Is it my heart? I can't tell. Try and look around I can't move my head and my eyes show nothing but the feint glow above. I move my fingers, their sensation tells me I am touching my legs but my legs have no feeling. I try to call out but still no sound will come. The panic rises again what can I do… it will eat me…. No…no go away? Close your eyes and think back, there is something, a memory, a dream, no matter think on. I see a face a face I don't know. A young face a girl? no a woman in gold. An angel? Am I dead? No I must be alive. The face moves closer I can feel warm breath and a sweet sickly smell invades my senses. I open my eyes. Nothing. I close my eyes again still nothing. I try to recall the face but it has gone the smell remains and it suddenly feels warmer.

Jane Thornby, the night duty paramedic had seen many Road Traffic Accidents (RTA) before although this was a little different. She and her partner Joe had extracted the patient from the passenger seat of the crashed car that had apparently driven into the back of a parked truck on the Alton Road.

There was no sign of the driver. Strange, as the driver's door was shut tight as was the passenger side and both airbags deployed. Where was the driver? To gain access Jane had to smash the rear window with a pointed hammer, supplied with their emergency kit for just such a situation. She cleared away most of the safety glass from the rear seat onto the floor, climbed in and reached through to release the passenger door by its inside handle. The passenger seat belt and air bag had saved her from the worst but she was unconscious and unresponsive. She checked the patient over and could find no physical damage, her pulse was shallow but steady enough, she moved closer to check her breathing. It was regular and there were no apparent broken bones or obvious head trauma. What was going on? She needed to get her to Basingstoke General as soon as possible. Jane and Joe secured her, a young woman in her twenties, to the stretcher then covered her with a blanket to protect her from the cold whilst Joe moved the trolley to the ambulance.

Jane quickly looked in the car for information on the young woman's identity. There was no sign of a handbag and the glove box was either locked or jammed shut.

The lone policemen had arrived a little after the ambulance, had parked with warning lights flashing to help secure the area and was speaking to the two witnesses. He moved over to the car and spoke to Jane. "Hello there I picked up the call on my car radio and as I was near by. I came to see if there was anything I could do, the traffic police should be here I don't know why not.

He looked over at the patient " Is she badly hurt?"

"I don't know yet, there is no obvious trauma, maybe just shock, we must get her to A and E now"

"Sure, I'll stay here until traffic arrives, I'll call and find out where they are"

She asked the officer if he would look for and bring any information to the hospital, as she did not want to delay any longer.

"By the way is there any sign of the driver?" She asked.

"I don't know" the officer replied, "The witnesses didn't see much or anyone leave the car, anyway they arrived some time after the incident and called us on their mobile. I thought she was the driver. Why do you ask?"

"There is something very wrong here" Jane offered "Please meet me at the hospital when you have finished up, my name is Jane Thornby, and please check further as this girl wasn't driving"

"It may be that we need and Accident Investigation Unit to attend, I will have to clear it with my sergeant first but I will check and get back to you then. I'm constable Andrews by the way. Why do you think she wasn't driving?

"We extracted her from the passenger seat unconscious, I can't talk now as I must go, please do what you can."

Peter Andrews went back to his car to find out where the traffic police were. The on-call unit had been sent to a major incident on the A303 so would not be there soon. He was ordered to deal with situation until another unit could be sent out.

The couple who had stopped and reported the accident were anxious to leave so Peter questioned them in more detail. They arrived on the scene soon after the accident had occurred saw no one or nothing to suggest that there was another driver. They did see a lone motor bike travelling in the opposite direction but no other vehicles on this little used road. He took their details and thanking them for their help allowed them to leave.

Chapter 2

Peter Andrews was not used to mysteries. It was just over two years since becoming a beat copper and as such only dealt as second string to his 'anything for a quiet' life sergeant who's main concern was getting home on time. He knew if he mentioned the paramedic's misgivings he would be put off by telling him not to worry him with her concerns and to leave it to the professionals. He had to play it carefully before he spoke to the boss.

He tried the driver's door it seemed it had been jammed shut by the accident and no amount of pulling would open it. "No way a driver exited that way". He thought, "she must have been driving and crawled over to the passenger side before collapsing. There can be no other explanation." He would find the girls handbag and then go to the hospital. He would casually tell the sergeant that he was going to the hospital with the girl's belongings and to see how she was getting on. He would also need to ask the hospital for an alcohol test.

He knew that his sergeant would leave that to him as it often involved a lot of hanging about. He then called Sergeant Mann and was told that DCI Bean ordered him to arrange for an Accident Investigation team before the car was to be cleared away.

He decided to investigate further whilst waiting for traffic to arrive, put on his neoprene gloves before he searched the car. He carefully took the key from the ignition using its edges only so as not to disturb any prints noting that the ignition was off. The key did not fit the glove box which he thought unusual. He carefully replaced the key to its original position. "That's odd I must note that in my report" he thought. He looked everywhere including having to break open the glove box. No bag, no ID. Again strange. He would use the car registration to find the owner from DVLA as soon as he got back to the station.

The traffic police unit arrived and appologised to him for the delay. He apprised them of the situation and what he had done. Their sergeant said " You should have waited for us constable, I will call the accident investigation unit if I considered it necessary. It is my decision to make and not yours."

Peter stood his ground and not wanting to be put down replied "Please contact Detective Chief Inspector Bean as the order to call them in came from him. I have to leave now if is there anything else I will be available at the station tomorrow."

Peter turned not waiting for a reply and went to his car. He wanted to follow up by interviewing the accident victim without telling the traffic police who were obviously not too happy with his interference in what they considered to be their territory.

He went directly to the hospital and looked around the ambulance station to try and find Jane the paramedic, only to be informed she was out on another call. He said to let her know he was in the hospital and needed to speak to her. He then asked the supervisor for the girl's location. He was directed to the ward C3 on the second floor.

He went upstairs to the wards and on to C3's nurse's station where the girl had been taken. He explained to the staff nurse on duty that he had been unable to obtain an identity, as yet, but would let them know when he did.

"How is she, has she regained consciousness?"

"Not yet, her condition is stable. We are doing blood tests and a scan which should help us find out what is wrong."

He asked would an alcohol level would be recorded from the blood tests. The nurse told him that would be done as a matter of course. He thanked them and left his number for them to contact him when she came round.

"Thanks I'll come by tomorrow anyway if that's all right."

Peter then left to go downstairs to see if he could find the paramedic Jane and also to get a coffee.

Chapter 3

I'm warm now but still can't move. The light is different brighter but still no images. I can hear voices but no words, this place is different. Where am I ? Who am I? Mary my name is Mary? That doesn't feel right. Why can't I move? I must ask Harriet when I see her.....Who is Harriet? I can't think straight. Close your eyes and relax. The smell comes again. I can see the face, no it's a different face this time, I know this face but who is it? Harriet, Mary? No I'm Mary or am I Harriet, what is going on in my head. I can't think straight.

'Try and Sleep' who said that? A soft voice again 'Try and Sleep'.... I will.

Constable Andrews found the café was not open at this late hour so had to settle for a lukewarm excuse for a coffee from a vending machine close to the A and E waiting room. He was sitting in the corridor gazing into his cup thinking of the oddities of the situation when Jane turned the corner just behind where he was sitting. She didn't notice him at first as his back was to her. He heard her voice and rose from his reverie to find her looking grave.

"Miss Thornby" he said "I've been to see the girl but no real news on her condition yet. Oh and I couldn't find any of her belongings in the car, perhaps someone else took them? Your partner perhaps?"

"No, that's not possible. I was first on the scene; Joe was getting the equipment when I went to the car. I can't believe there was no ID of any kind"

"Miss Thornby, I ...." She interrupted him "Please call me Jane"

"Ok, Jane, I examined the car, as you know the doors were shut tight so she must have been the driver and climbed over after the accident"

Jane was not convinced "I don't see how that can be, she was strapped in with her air bag deployed, no one could have climbed over with the airbag like that. The drivers airbag was also deployed?"

"Yes" said Peter "but it had deflated when I examined the car"

Jane was incredulous "So she would have had to disconnect her seat belt climb past her air bag, over the center console in to the passenger seat, moving by the passenger airbag, clip in the passenger seatbelt and reposition the airbag, all before going into a coma. No way"

" I don't know it's a mystery for sure" Peter was not convinced either way. "Perhaps the driver climbed out over her or even locked the car when he left."

"Not without moving the airbag and that was in position still partially inflated when I got there. To lock the car before leaving he would need to have had a second key, unlikely and why do that? Habit maybe.....No this is not right" Jane was thinking out loud "What are you going to do?"

"I'm not sure. I'll need to think about this a bit longer. Did she drive or is there a third party involved? Oh, another odd thing the ignition key did not fit the glove box so I had to break it open to look for ID. I'm inclined to think the driver did a runner and took her belongings with him. I'm going back to the station now to try and find out who she is through the car data. I'll speak to my boss again I hope the traffic police have informed the Accident Investigation Unit (AIU) to attend the scene. Give me your mobile number and I'll call you when I have some news" Jane gave him her number and he left.

Jane and Joe were then sent out on another call, so had to leave. On their return they were close to the end of their shift. Jane hoped they would not be called out again as she wanted to find out about the girl's condition.

Jane didn't normally get involved once the patients had been delivered to A and E as mostly they were either on their way to the morgue or awake and on the mend before her shift had finished. This was different. Too many unknowns and one apparent impossibility, a car that drove itself into the back of a truck. Although Jane's shift was about to end she couldn't get the young girl out of her mind so before she changed to go home she went up to the ward to see how she was faring. The doctor on duty Mike Smith was a third year intern whom Jane had met on several occasions when he was on out-duty call. "Hello doctor any news here?"

"No change" he replied "I presume you were the one who brought her in"

"Yes" said Jane "but it was strange the circumstances of her accident though" She explained what had happened and the anomaly of the missing driver. "There was so little trauma, how come she is in such a deep coma?"

"Well there was certainly no head damage that we could see, but it could just have been the shock that caused her to shut down. Her BP and vitals are all normal so I don't think she is in any danger. She hasn't had a scan as yet, that's scheduled for tomorrow morning. We were waiting for an ID and some medical history before we went any further. Oh and I'm expecting the blood results, they should have been here by now. Do you think the police have found out who she is yet?"

"I don't know. The constable at the scene said he would call me when he had some news, in any case he should inform the hospital of her name and address as a matter of course. I expect he will be coming here to see her for a statement when she comes round."

Jane was wondering why Peter hadn't called already; he should have traced the girl through the car number plate by now.

"Goodnight Dr. Smith. I'll be on late duty tomorrow. I'll come by before I start work"

"Goodbye Jane, I'll let you know if there are any changes"

Jane walked to the locker room still wondering what was going on. She put on her day clothes and went to her car. At this time of the morning there were few cars in the car park and little traffic, so she would be home in less than twenty minutes.

Jane was born in Basingstoke, on 12th October 1988, to Susan and David. An older stepbrother and younger sister had long ago left home leaving Jane with Mum and Dad. She recently decided to move away and now shared a cottage in Bramley Village with Pam, a nurse who also worked at the hospital, and their landlord Pam's cousin Charlie.

Jane was a little over weight, in fact she appeared quite dumpy despite her not too short 5 ft. 5 inch frame. Although she tried to eat sensibly the job left her often with little choice, fast food or nothing.

Her ambition of becoming a nurse never materialized, as she couldn't settle to the college education required. Becoming a paramedic seemed to be second best initially but she soon grew to love its challenges and variety. Now recognized by her peers as one of the good ones she was quick and accurate in her assessment of her patients needs.

She loved the idea of driving her own ambulance, but although she had passed her driving test first time failed to meet the standards required by the ambulance service. You were only given one shot at that test. Jane never understood why she had failed, they never told her, but suspected she was over zealous, perhaps a little dangerous. She had come to be almost glad that she had failed, as she would not have been partnered with Joe otherwise. He and she had become a magic team and he and his family her best friends. Jane had light brown thick straight hair that she kept short, her dark complexion and round face gave her a young boyish look that belied her twenty-nine years. She was never going to be thin but was fit and very strong. She liked to walk for exercise, hated running but would jog occasionally, if time were short.

Charlie worked in London. He commuted daily from Basingstoke station and was getting ready to leave just as Jane arrived home. This was a regular crossing of paths when Jane was on nights.

They exchanged a “Hello” “Goodbye” with the usual little laugh of familiarity. Pam wasn’t home yet her duties seldom coincided with Jane’s so she had the cottage to herself. She suddenly felt exhausted so didn’t even bother with food or a shower and went straight to bed.

Although she was tired out daytime sleeping was always difficult. Her blackoout curtains helped but the strange events of the night before kept her mind active for some time before she drifted off.

Chapter 4

Peter Andrews arrived at the police station in the center of town at ten pm. The squad room was almost deserted just the night sergeant and one other officer. Sergeant Fred Mann had signed out and gone home leaving Peter to do the paperwork as always. He didn't mind as he enjoyed his personal space and unlike some other PCs here he had no one breathing down his neck all the time.

P.C. Peter James Andrews stood six feet one inch, he was proud of that inch, twelve stone and the newest member of Basingstoke's police team.

Brought up on a Downham estate in south London his parents were keen for him to be well educated. His father was a carpenter, not ambitious but highly skilled, he worked for the same local building company all his life. Their home was cared for by his Mum, she did all the things that mums do and still does to this day. He went to a local comprehensive school and sixth form college where he had very good A level grades. He always wanted to be a policeman ever since listening to fantastic tales told by his great uncle Nobby who was a retired London detective. The stories were exagerated for effect but the impression on young Peter was fundamental in his desire to follow in Nobby's footsteps.

He had wanted to join up as soon as he left school but was persuaded by his Dad and the police recruitment officer that he should go to university first. He reluctantly agreed and made several applications for a place. Once he had a place offered at London University he warmed to the idea.

Three years later a graduate of West London College, with a second-class honours degree in Math's under his belt; he worked his way through the Hendon Police College course with a class of fellow graduates, now realizing that the anticipated glamour expounded by his late uncle, of being a policeman was a myth. All paperwork and repetition. He accepted the monotony as the means to achieving his burning ambition of becoming a detective.

He had been assigned to assist Sergeant Fred Mann who in turn reported to Detective Chief Inspector Craig Bean. Fred was of an age where retirement loomed and although he was of the 'Old

School' did not appear to resent 'fast tracked graduates' achieving promotion that had passed him by.

As an ordinary constable Peter wore the uniform, unlike Sergeant Mann. Although he was attached to the detectives he hadn't yet been given the promotion to detective constable. Peter was living in the police house adjacent to the station, accommodation shared with two other officers, which suited him fine. Their different shifts meant they hardly met,

As all three were tidy enough domestic clashes never occurred unlike when he was in university.

He was the tidy one, living with five guys who had never heard of houswork and didn't intend to start finding out was a strain. He survived by being tollerant in the extreme but was glad for the vacations and the end of three years being housemaid to his temporary mates. It had improved the last year when one of the lads left and was repaced by a young girl who at least kept the washing up under control.

On days off he would either visit his parents in SE London or his sister in Southampton. Mum's Sunday roast was a seldom-achievable highlight lately.

Peter sat down at his computer to enter his report, remembering that he needed to find out who the victim was and also to try and resolve the 'who was the driver' problem. He logged on to the special police DVLA link and entered the Golf's registration number. Up popped the name and address of the keeper. David Kidd, 23, Paradise Close Kempshot. The VW Golf was taxed, insured and had a current MOT.

The house was on a Basingstoke estate just fifteen minutes from the station. He searched further to see that David his wife Alison and their daughter Melanie were drivers at that address.

Peter paused and thought what to do next. It would normally be Sergeant Mann's duty to follow up this and go to the house but in order not to delay Peter took it upon himself. "Could the victim be Melanie?" I seemed likely and he was sure the parents were unaware of what had happened. He hated this task it was always fraught with maximum anxiety and often included traumatic breakdowns. This was a visit that shouldn't be done when alone so he went to the duty sergeant to see who was available at so late an hour. There was a car with a WPC on patrol that was recalled by the desk sergeant to take him to the house in Kempshot.

Chapter 5

Fred Mann arrived home earlier than usual, glad that young Peter was very capable of dealing with a simple road accident. Fred was born in Basingstoke and had lived there almost all his life. He went to school there, married and had brought up their family in the same village.

He joined the police as a cadet. Now in his late fifties he had been eligible for retirement for some time but had chosen to stay on. Married to Fiona for more than thirty years he had lately taken to looking after her more and more as her health had declined.

Their son Topper (a nickname due to his thick dark hair from a baby) lived and worked up north so the burden was all on Fred. Topper had gone to university in York to study engineering. He had met and fell in love with Josephine a student a year younger than him. After graduating he came home and stayed for a while leaving Jo to finish her final year at college. Topper had not found work locally although not throught the lack of trying. Applications made to many companies produce few results but was eventually offered an interview with

Shell Oil who offered him a job as a trainee in pipeline construction. He was over the moon but it required a move to Aberdeen in Scotland. Fred and Fiona were sad to see him go but promises of frequent visits mollfied the hurt they were feeling. He had returned home only once during the first six months. During his visit he explained that he and Jo wanted to get married when she had finished her studies and he had found a house just outside Aberdeen where they would live.

The wedding took place a year later in a small church in the village where they had both settled. Fred and Fiona went to the event and met Jo and her family for the first time. They were delighted for their son as they were a lovely family and Jo was all they could have wished for.

They knew then that they would see very little of their son as Topper had established a life and new friends in Scotland that would grow strong over the coming years. The promises to visit were once again made but without conviction.

Fiona's MS had worsened over the last two years requiring day and sometimes night care which were eating into their savings which would not last for ever. There was no way he could afford professional help on a pension, hence his forced continued employment, retirement just a dream.

He had been a diligent if unambitious copper who had worked long hours over many years so felt no guilt about taking time off now and again to be with Fiona. Young Andrews was keen and efficient so made up for Fred's present shortcomings.

Peter was well aware of Fred's domestic problems, as was everyone at the station, so even the DCI and Super turned a sympathetic blind eye.

In the days when Fred joined the police things were less formal, after the initial period of 'on the job training' which meant making the tea and being a fetch and carry boy for the officers in Basingstoke station, he was sent to Hendon for the real basic training course. He did well enough and was stationed in Camberwell, south London for the first period of service. His life as a policeman in London was far from what he had expected. Most of his colleagues in the force were always looking for ways to gain an advantage. His superiors only wanted results and didn't seem to care how they achieved them. He did his best to do what was, in his opinion, the right way but inevitably the pressure to get results left him consorting with the less savoury element of society and sometimes bending the rules. It was not his fault but corrupt practice had been just the way it was. He longed to be back home but his several applications for a posting to Hampshire were ignored for some time but eventually his request was granted and much to his delight was sent back to Basingstoke.

He had seen life in London for nearly two years and had no desire to remain there and even less to raise a family in such an environment.

Fred had met Fiona before he moved to London, childhood sweethearts almost, and although being together was a bit on and off he still went home and often saw her on his leave days. Once back in home territory their relationship blossomed leading to their eventual marriage. When their son Topper came along Fred's life was complete. He made Sergeant after a few years of steady service and was happy with his cosy uncomplicated lot.

That was the case for many happy years until Fiona developed Multiple Sclerosis.

Freds life changed from then on, slowly at first as the progression of the disease was gradual and Fiona could still do most household chores. She was stubborn to the point where she insisted to go shopping on her own for a while, untill the inevitable happened, she had a fall and couldn't get up. From then on it was downhill leading to the wheelchair as the only means of mobility outside the home. There was some help from the NHS and the Multiple Sclerosis Society, but they could not provide the twenty four hour coverage needed. This meant Fred either had to pay for carers to cover the periods when he was working or leave Fiona alone. Much of the time this was fine as the council paid for day visits that allowed him to work without worry. The night duties were more difficult. He would help her to bed before going out, leaving her with a mobile phone that was her lifeline to a private care company who would respond if needed.

The guys at work were real good and covered him whenever they could but her needs had gradually increased. If he retired he would have less need for help but knew he could not cope on his own and the pension would hardly cover professional help.

Chapter 6

Peter, along with WPC June Owens, were on the doorstep of number 23. "Don't like this one bit" moaned Peter. "It has to be done though" June replied.

He reluctantly rang the bell, with no immediate response he tried again and also knocked. After a couple more knocks a light went on in an upstairs room and the window opened.

"Excuse me sir are you Mr. Kidd" Peter voiced to the shadowy figure at the upstairs window.

"Yes. What the blazes do you want at this time of night?" came the disgruntled reply.

"It is the police sir, my name is Constable Andrews and this is WPC Owens. I need to speak to you urgently, if you could please come to the door sir it would be easier."

A few minutes later there was a rattling of locks at the door that opened slowly to the limit of the safety chain. When Mr. Kidd spied the uniform and the police car parked outside he undid the chain and opened the door fully,

"What do you want?"

"I am sorry to disturb you sir at this late hour but could I please come in?"

"I don't know, what's it about"

"Are you the owner of a Golf registration number DA12NNM?"

"Yes that's my car why what's wrong"

Peter again asked to come in whereupon Mr. Kidd ushered him into the front room.

"What is it David?" came a ladies voice from upstairs.

"Nothing dear" He said I'll be up in a minute.

"I think your wife should be here too" said Peter

Mr. Kidd called nervously to his wife to come down, which she did a few minutes later.

"Please sit down Mr. Kidd....Mrs. Kidd" Peter was getting anxious

"Is it my Mother?" said Mrs. Kidd "has something happened to her?"

"No no not that, I'm sorry to inform you that a short while ago your car was involved in an accident and a young lady passenger has been injured. She is stable and has been taken to Basingstoke hospital"

Immediately Mr. Kidd jumped up and shouted at Peter "You are crazy coming here like that getting us all worked up. Are you really sure? You've got it wrong somehow, please leave"

Peter was taken aback he had never had a reaction to bad news like this before "Calm down sir calm down, I can assure you this is no joke"

Another voice called from upstairs. "Dad. Mum what's going on down there?"

Mr. Kidd then stormed out into the hall and came back with a bunch of keys. Followed by a young girl. "Here are my keys" he said, "you will find my car in the garage."

"I'm sorry to upset you but would you please show me the car," said Peter recovering his composure from the sudden outburst. Seeing the daughter gave him cause for doubt. They all went to the front of the house and Mr. Kidd unlocked the up and over door. Peter expected to see an empty garage, thinking the car must have been stolen. But no. There it was a navy blue Golf registration number DA12NNM.

It took a while to calm the family down and to check the VIN vehicle identification number against the registration document and to take a statement from Mr. Kidd. "I'll never do that again, bloody fool, should have checked with the boss before blundering in like that, he won't be a happy man" more to himself than June Owens.

"At least it wasn't their daughter" she said

"No, but it still someone else's and we are no closer to finding whose"

They had learnt something significant however; it wasn't a stolen car but a false registration number fitted to an identical Golf. Another mystery. Peter groaned, this was going to be a long night stretching into a long day. He needed to assemble his thoughts and plan what needed to be done next before he woke Fred Mann from his just commenced slumber.

First things first he thought "Inform the AI guys of the facts so far and that the car and scene needed to be processed. Text the boss with an update, Lord knows how long the investigators would take."

All this still left the girl unidentified and a magician of a driver to find. He must get to the hospital to try and get a statement if possible and get a picture to assist with her ID. Before he left for the hospital he rang Fred Mann who told him to wait as it looked as if the chief would need to be involved.

Fred said he would deal with that and would send a message to DCI Bean.

Whilst he was waiting Peter called the paramedic Jane but got no reply. He sent a text telling her to call him when she could, as they were no nearer finding out who the girl was.

There was not much for Peter to do whilst he waited. The Chief had not contacted him niether had Sergeant Mann so he decided to go to the police house his now home and wait there. On his way out of the station he asked the duty sergeant to call him there if needed.

Chapter 7

Here I am. I have been asleep but although I know I am awake I am not. Where was I yesterday? Mary should be here too she was with me then so where has she gone? I had better tell Harriet to find her. I will. A light, so bright, who is there? Now it has gone. Come back please come back.

Jane awoke earlier than usual so she lay for a while remembering the strange day yesterday. She reached for her phone and saw the missed call from the policeman. Perhaps Peter had found out who she is. She was angry that she had slept through the ring. She then read her texts and realized that the call would not have resolved her questions but raised even more which no doubt would have kept her awake. She was grateful that her much needed sleep had not been disturbed. She was hungry and thirsty having missed her yesterday's pre-sleep snack so set about making a breakfast and coffee before calling Peter Andrews. Jane loved her breakfasts it was the only meal she had control over. Even though it was often taken in the afternoon she still prepared eggs bacon and beans or sometimes tomatoes with toast and butter. Today it was beans. The preparation of the meal gave her time to awaken fully, late shifts made sleeping difficult, it also played havoc with your social life not that she had much of that anyway.

Mike Smith came on duty at midday, the start of a twelve or fourteen hour shift. Tired before he started he boosted his resolve with the thought of his future as a senior registrar and eventually consultant. A long haul but he was over the worst, the long hours were a given for all young doctors, as long as he could survive the constant fatigue he was becoming more experienced and his diagnostic skills were being recognized by his peers and even his mentor would occasionally listen and agree with his opinion.

Mike a tall, heavy set; fair-haired man was determined to find out what was wrong with this young girl.

Today Mike Smith would carry on as always, moving slowly one step nearer his 'golden stethoscope'

Miss unknown had not moved. Mike checked her pulse, temperature, blood pressure and respiration then listened to her heart. The monitors were all functioning fine. He then examined her skin for signs of latent bruising which may have not been visible the night before especially around he neck and back. He noticed the inside of her right thigh had several dark spots almost out of sight unless you looked closely. " Are these injection bruises?" he was puzzled "No seat belt mark of any kind, "unusual" he thought, "must have been spared that little trauma by the airbag." There were no jerk responses and she seemed impervious to small pain using pinpricks. The only reaction to stimuli were her eyes where the pupils responded to light as expected. She would follow the light in all directions. No response to sound. Could something other than her accident have caused this? Externally she seems fine.

He observed her saline drip it was ok. What had happened to this young person to cause her to shut down her nervous system? He needed to have that scan done now even if there is no medical history, there must be spinal or neurological damage not obvious to the eye.

He called the lab for the blood results to be told they were still not ready and to give them another two hours. Angry at the delay he yelled down the phone "What are you doing down there? I should have had these yesterday!... Err No ..I'm sorry I didn't mean that it's just that I really do need these results... sorry again ..when you can ok" He hung up frustrated and annoyed at his outburst. There was no use chivvying them along as they were overloaded like everyone here. He felt frustrated that he could do no more.

She was almost comatose physically although thankfully she was breathing well without assistance. He looked down at her young and pretty face; her eyes partly open feeling the same was not feeking so well mentally.

He moved closer and gently spoke "Can you see me, can you hear me, we are here for you?" Nothing. Perhaps when Mr. Lawson came on he would have an idea in any case they would have the blood-work and the scan results by then. "This is silly I mustn't get so involved" he said to himself irritated. "Attend to your other patients" with that self-rebuke he reluctantly moved to the nurses' station.

Jane decided to drive to work before making the call, she hoped it would be a quiet morning and as she had left early in spite of the delay in consuming her hearty breakfast, she would have twenty or so minutes before her duty started. The fact that she was not officially on duty would make no difference if an emergency call came in. As long as her partner and driver Joe was there they would be sent out anyway. She may also have time to enquire about the girl's condition. As it happened Joe Felix was not there when she arrived so she called Peter's mobile. He answered almost straight away. "Hi, thanks for getting back to me, how is the patient, has she come round?"

"I don't know I have only just arrived at work; I'll go and see in a minute. What news do you have? Have you found out who she is yet?"

Peter then went on to explain what had happened with the Kidd family. He didn't mention his embarrassment with Mr. Kidd and his surprise that the car's identity had been stolen. He kept his account very matter of fact. He told her how the forensic expert would examine the wreck and find the original VIN (vehicle identity number). Even if the identity plate had been removed there were other places, like the engine, where unique numbers were more difficult to remove. He told her that in any case the wrecked car was most likely stolen so would only lead to the real owner and probably a blind alley with regards to identifying the patient.

"Will I see you later" Peter asked almost shyly.

"Maybe. Will you be at the hospital tonight?"

"I could be. You're on night shift aren't you, I just work when I have to, usually early mornings and late nights?"

"I know, no time for anything much. Officially we're doing six till two this month but we are short staffed so we could be on all night if it's busy."

"Look I'll be coming into the hospital when I've finished here to check on the girl anyway so I'll look for you then"

"We might be on call, if I'm not here ring me tomorrow"

"Ok Jane see you bye" Peter close his phone.

Chapter 8

The RTA team had finished the examination of the site, photos taken measurements made, interviews and statements taken from the witnesses. They had been unable to traced the owner of the truck, a half cab Transit pick up that appeared to have broken down earlier that day. Green Flag had been called but were unable to help at the scene as the truck was deserted and locked when they got there. Green Flag did not have the truck registered and would not tow the vehicle away until the driver contacted them with his membership details. This had not happened, no one knew why.

There were a number of strange anomalies for which Henry Jakes, the team leader, could not find an answer.

Road traffic accidents or incidents as they are now known, always threw up unknowns but there were too many things here that did not jibe with Henry.

There were no skid marks. The truck had been pushed well off the road with only the driver's side wheels just on the carriageway. A warning Triangle had been deployed well in advance about 30meters behind the truck. The hazard warning light switch had been turned on, although at the time of the examination the battery was flat, so not conclusive that they were visible at the time of the incident. Neither of the witnesses remembered seeing hazard lights.

The damage to the car and truck was central and slight suggesting a low speed impact but obviously hard enough to trigger the air bags. Strangest of all the warning triangle still intact, untouched as if the car had swerved into the truck after passing the warning, either that or the triangle had been placed there after which seems very unlikely. Lastly expecting to find the driver's door jammed because of the impact discovered that it was in fact just locked. This with the keys still in the ignition in the off position seemed very odd indeed. The PC had left a note explaining the broken glass also the damaged glove box and what he done with the key. Henry wished the PC had waited before removing the key but understood his reasons. He thought it would be ok and hoped the constable had not compromised any evidence.

Henry sighed, "Too many unknowns here, not right, definitely not right" He arranged for the car and truck to be picked up and taken to the RTA compound at Alton where he would be able to examine both vehicles more thoroughly to better understand what had happened. At the moment he was at a loss.

He called Fred Mann to give him heads up on what he knew so far. He was sure that Fred would want to follow up yet again with the witnesses and truck owner, if he could find him, whilst their memories were still fresh. Henry had not had the chance to speak to Fred or his constable so was unaware that the car had been stolen and ringed.

It was after 11pm by the time Henry had finished. Fred did not answer his phone and the duty sergeant at the station said constable Andrews was not there he decided to call it a day and follow up in the morning.

Henry's team was already at work when he arrived at the vehicle examination area.

PC Andrews had informed them of the duplicated number plates and that it was probably stolen. He also gave them the real car's details not knowing if that would help their task or not.

The car had been partially stripped; the seats were out, the bonnet and boot lid removed. All Henry could see were an unidentified pair of legs protruding from under the body and the unmistakable rear end of Joe Riley with his head in the engine bay.

"Hello guv" came from Mary Bailey who stood up from behind the car as he approached. "A real pro job here, everything's been removed or ground down, we'll have to do an acid test on the engine block to even have a chance of an ident on this one." Just then Mark Charley slid out from under the chassis with a big smile on his face. "No luck here with numbers boss, they've all been removed but I've found several prints on the chassis and one full hand where they must have pulled themselves out from under."

"Good job Mark" said Henry as he removed his overcoat. "Load them up in the computer and we'll see if these fellows are legit or bad guys we have met before. It amazes me they go to all the trouble of grinding off the numbers and then go and leave a personal 'printed' calling card."

"Morning Hen.." said Joe as he lifted his head from under the bonnet waving the car's computer in his hand.

"They always leave something for us to find. They've changed the steering lock; must have bust it when the car was stolen; but did not bother with the electronics. Central locking code does not match the key, hence the locked doors. Another mistake the key itself had been wiped but they have forgotten the fob, a nice thumb and index finger there"

'Well done guys, you can get to the truck later this afternoon but concentrate on the car for now, with these prints we may get lucky. Joe can you extract the central locking code and any other identifying numbers from the computer we may be able to match it to a particular vehicle"

Henry did not hold out much hope from that as VW records are difficult to trace especially the Golf. There are so many and they are made all over the place; unless you knew where the car was manufactured it was a needle in a haystack task.

He left his team to get on with their work and went to his office. Six e-mails and two call outs for site visits. “Hardly have time for a cuppa” he thought “Needs must…” On the way out he collard Mary. “May, you’ll have to leave that you’re coming with me we’ve a three car shunt on the ring road. Traffic needs us to find out who’s at fault.”

“ Mary stood waving her greasy hands “ Here we go again, give us a minute to clean up and get my gear, see you outside in two shakes”

“You two finish the car then give the truck the once over. Let Chief Beanpole know if you find anything significant. I’ll call you when we’re done”

“Okedokay Hen” The two replied in practiced unison.

“Pair of joker twins you are” Henry ‘tut-tutted’ on his way out. He wouldn’t have it any other way it kept them sane from a task that often involved delving into terrible traggic scenes.

Chapter 9

Harriet Mary Fairchild had been a research assistant at Dun and Bradstreet for five years. She was supposedly on two weeks leave, living it up in Rhodes, at least that is what her friends and colleagues thought, instead she was lying unconscious in a hospital bed miles from her home and office. She was not going to be reported missing for days yet.

Harriet was bored, she wanted more than to be studying files and financial record of companies she had never heard of. The work was well paid but tedious and uninteresting. Although she adhered strongly to the company ideals of truth and meaning in her reports, her accountancy degree was little used and did nothing to inspire her inquisitive mind. Along with the rapid advance in technology came a new generation of techno-criminals who were daily relieving their unsuspecting victims of their hard earned cash. She dearly wanted to become involved in discovering what enabled these thieves to flourish and to stop them from enjoying such easy pickings.

This desire came about when she became personally part of a scheme using the Internet to steal money when she attended a four-day seminar on 'Investment Law' sponsored by London University. She had seen an advertisement on her email with links to a website giving details of that particular course along with others. The presenters proposed were well known and the syllabus to her liking. She requested an application, which duly arrived in the post. The fee was £400, which she knew would be refunded to her from D & B's training budget, so filled out the form and sent off her cheque. She could also have paid on line if she wanted, which she found out later many candidates had done. A few days later venue details arrived along with her receipt.

The day she arrived at the venue there was chaos, the room allocated was too small with not enough of seats for even half the attendees. The course coordinator checked people's receipts finding them seemingly all in order. She managed to quiet everyone down apologizing for the delay stating

"I will move us all to a larger room, if you would be so kind as to wait in the hall here I will see to it."

Some fifteen minutes later she returned and led us along the hall up the stairs to a lecture hall large enough by a long way as it would seat more than a hundred.

Once seated the head count was forty five, she had only twelve registered to attend, which was strange as between forty and fifty was more normal for these events. She would contact her office later to find out what had gone wrong. She introduced the first day Lecturer again apologizing for the mix up and delay.

Harriet was two days into the seminar when she spied the coordinator at lunch in the college refectory.

“Hello again, I’m Harriet I’m on your Investment Law course, it is very good. By the way what went wrong with the numbers, a bit embarrassing but you handled it well?”

“Oh hi, I’m Megan Bayliss” pointing at her lapel name badge “I thought it was my mistake at first or one of the office girls but no. Keep this to yourself but we have been scammed.” Megan was dying to share her story. ”I had twelve on my list there were thirty-three extras what a shambles wasn't it. Oh...a bit odd.. One of mine did not turn up either"

It transpired that a website had been created identical to the official one with the exception of the price this being lower at £250. The new false site had been prioritized to the top page of the search engine relegating the official page way down the list. The false site at first glance was no different so the alteration went unnoticed.

Applications had been sent out to those enquirers with return address (a PO Box number)) and payment details very different to the real ones. The price difference was set to attract would be clients away from the official site. Clever that, lots of £250 being better than just a few £400. One of the genuine candidates who did not attend was the one who gained all the information needed to duplicate the application form and receipts. When they checked he had used the same PO Box that no longer existed.

Over eight thousand pounds had been deposited and withdrawn, the account closed, website shut down. All in the space of a few days and virtually untraceable. London University had honoured the extra attendees in order to preserve their reputation.

Megan had heard that other seminars had been attacked in this way not just London colleges but she didn't know how many. They sponsor at least twenty such courses in a year, which made Harriet think how could the hijackers, get away with this so easily. Over a hundred thousand pounds or maybe more for a few hours at a keyboard. She resolved to investigate.

All that was some time ago, Harriet had attended many more courses concentrating on improving her computer knowledge and studying Internet crimes relating to accountancy and fraud. Her skill and reputation had grown whereupon she left Dun and Bradstreet to join a small Government sponsored company of like-minded people. At last Harriet had found her niche.

Chapter 10

Toby Cutler-Jones was not what you would expect with a name like that. Lean but muscular, tallish at six foot. His face was pale, some childhood chickenpox scarring on his cheeks, dark hair kept short but well styled. His hands and nails were well groomed with short fingers nearly always curled in a fist. His south London accent still persisted despite his trying to maintain a different persona. He wasn't vain but dressed well, guided by others in what was fashionable and of the best quality. He didn't like suits but wore them as a uniform required by his trade, deception and manipulation. When at home he was either in shorts and T-shirt or jeans and jumper.

He was born in Peckham thirty-nine years ago as David Charles Jones, David chosen by Mum and Charles after his Dad Charlie. David Jones at birth but because of his stick out '*Toby jug*' ears from a baby he had been nicknamed Toby. He didn't mind the nickname even though the source of its origin was a family joke. His ears didn't bother him in fact was proud of the nickname they had given rise to;

he liked his bit of 'posh'. He adopted the add-on Cutler much later when he wished to impress clients looking to invest in his property empire. The second eldest with one older sister and three younger brothers, his mother and father were kind and loving providing a clean if poor home for him and his siblings.

Peckham was a tough place to grow up. You became street wise real quick or your life was going to be difficult. He was a scrapper from early on where many a split lip and busted nose were inflicted on those who crossed him. His friends were just as unforgiving such that their reputation protected him and them from all other would be top dogs on the estate.

He was an intelligent lad with a desire to learn, finding school lessons a great stimulus especially economics. Most teachers liked him for his attentiveness as very few of his fellow students showed interest in anything but themselves. His desire to learn meant they often turned a blind eye to his sometimes-belligerent behavior. He was adept at ingratiating himself with all manner of people to his advantage.

He left school at sixteen with five 'O' levels, much to the sadness of his teachers who wanted him to stay on; university material was thin on the ground in Peckham. Not for him, he left and never looked back; he'd learnt enough there and wanted to get on with discovering and living in the real World.

He secured a job at Maseby's Estate Agents nearby as an assistant to the manager. Basically he made the tea and did the filing. He kept his head down, did all that was asked of him gradually learning the trade and gaining favour from his boss by anticipating his every need and working extra hours without pay delivering documents by hand to the various clients in the area. He opened read, then resealed these letters occasionally gaining useful information about the contracts or clients that he stored away for future reference. The agent/negotiators selling the houses were paid low wages making the bulk of their income from sales commission. There were great rivalries among the four who worked at Masby's. Whenever prospective clients came in while all the agents were out Toby would take their details but instead of putting them on file for distribution by the manager he would covertly pass them on to one or other of the agents depending upon who would be most financially grateful. He found later that one of the agents would keep the client to himself and do a deal with the customer direct. This turned out to be a very lucrative arrangement for him too as he now had this agent in his pocket and a large share of the fees. The money was useful but he more liked the power he now had over someone other than himself. He moved around London from one agency to another building up his experience and acquiring a number of like-minded friends in the business. At the age of twenty-three he had enough money, confidence and contacts to put his grand plan into action.

Under the name of David Charles Agents he leased four ground floor rooms in a virtually deserted old engineering works in Paul Street, Shoreditch. He had the vision that this old building in the City of London would become part of the growth explosion of the twenty first century and he wanted to be in the thick of it.

Bowlers Ltd was a small private company who had leased the building to an electrical engineering company and had enjoyed a good rental income for many years for little effort. The electrical firm declined to renew their lease two years previously and moved to a new town site. Bowers problems began. Short lets since had done little but prolong the agony.

Toby had done his homework, knew they were short of cash with demands for business rates, and maintenance bills growing they were glad of Toby's up front payment and his promise to take on more as his business grew. With threatening bankruptcy they were clutching at straws. Apart from Toby the building was now deserted and ripe and ready for picking.

Two phone lines, a fax, a Xerox copy machine, a desk and a chair were all he needed to conquer this part of the World. The time was approaching to call together those influential friends, those that he had made a lot of money on his journey through the property market place. They owed him and now the time to call in those debts was here.

In a private lounge of the Regent Palace Hotel he had called a meeting of these 'near friends' to explain his plan. Five guys with money and influence who had all benefited considerably from Toby's help in the past and he knew that whatever he had in mind they were there to a man for a piece of the pie.

"Gentlemen today we will begin to rebuild this city and in the process you and I will make a lot of money. Are you with me?"

So began the empire building of Toby C Jones. World Wide Enterprises was born.

W.W. Enterprises offered to buy the rundown Shoreditch building at a price that Bowlers' directors were reluctant to accept but Toby knew they really couldn't refuse. Vacant possession was required to close the deal. There was the small problem of the tenant 'David Charles.' Toby accepted the ten grand offered by the Bowers MD to give up his lease, a nice little bonus that he kept to himself, the big bucks were yet to come. The sale went through he was now MD of W.W. Enterprises Ltd. His dream of an empire had begun.

Within six months planning for a twenty-story office complex was granted, the old building demolished and construction commenced at 100 Paul Street.

Chapter 11

"Sandra we bloody well have to do something about that damn Fairchild bitch she is getting too close." said Toby in a gruff impatient voice. Pacing up and down behind his large desk empty except for the report that had triggered his emotional outburst. When his accounts office flagged up that enquiries had been made by a government agency concerning some finacial transfers made by Toby he had his private detective Joe Mallard look into where they had come from.

"I know! I know! What can we do? She could be on to us already"

"Not according to this, she has not made the link yet or we would know about it already. The surveyor has been well paid and gone away overseas on holiday. Before he left he destroyed all paper records of his visit and has deleted any file relating to the site and us. She will be hard pressed to prove anything there"

"That's as may be, if she gets wind of the sale she could still go to the consortium with her suspicions even without proof."

Sandra jumped to a quick solution "We could eliminate her altogether for a price. I know someone." She said without any qualms.

"That would be foolish a dead girl who is investigating the Company and very probably me would surely lead back to us. That's a can of worms I don't want the police sniffing at. If only we could keep her out of harms way for a week or so the deal will be done. Too late for her to influence anything, the money will be long gone and so will we."

Toby had sold off many of the smaller properties owned by W.W. Some creative accounting had enabled him to salt away much of the cash into private offshore accounts.

The properties that were left were large but only produced a marginal income. Although the cash flow looked good and the asset values were high they only just covered the loans tied to them and maintenance. Long-term capital investments required patience, not a quality in Toby's makeup. The land development would have given the Company a huge boost but the only way out now was to sell W.W as soon as possible.

The sale of W.W. Enterprises Ltd. Was almost finalised. The European Consortium was completely unaware that the land primed for development could never be used. If revealed now the sale would fall through, W.W. would not survive the ensuing fallout.

Unusual for him, Toby jumped at the chance to buy such a prime piece of land without checking everything first. There were other interested purchasers whom he wanted to beat to the deal. The price was cheap enough for WW to buy and with the banks support he could do this without going public. He had never wanted to go public, as some of his associates would have liked, for he would never relinquish control. He had 75% of the Company shares so could do almost as he wished.

He knew the site had some old derelict buildings dating way back, which would strengthen their planning applications. Nothing showed up on the basic searches carried out by the firm's solicitors so Toby went ahead aware that with his 'friends' on the Council he would be able to build a huge development there.

The first surveys were good and the Council had been given positive indications that planning would be granted. He knew that throwing in some 'affordable housing' would sweeten the doubters not under his influence.

Then came the blow that shook him rigid. The land was contaminated. How bad he was yet to find out.

Knowing that there were problems with sewage and the high water table Toby wanted to be ahead of the game with solutions when it came to the official Council surveys being done. "Thank God I did this privately" Thought Toby phoning the surveyor to come to his office immediately.

William Rose an unassuming man in his thirties entered Toby's office a little nervously knowing that his report would have been a shock.

"Come in William sit down.... can I get you something... a coffee ...a juice perhaps?"

"No thank you sir" said William "I'm sorry about the report I wish it wasn't so bad"

"So do I....so do I" responded Toby smiling as if it was not a real problem. "Anyway we can deal with it I'm sure"

William then went into detail about the degree of contamination. Apparently it was originally a farm where the farmer and his son had been killed during the First World War leaving only a mother and children to inherit. The mother could not run the farm on her own and for a small payment, which to her was a lifeline, unwittingly allowed massive unofficial dumping of waste chemicals used in the iron and munitions industries prior to and during that war. There was no official record. The contamination had remained undetected as the site had eventually grown over and anyone who witnessed it had passed away. It remained unused ever since. The current owners had no interest in the land and wanted to sell completely unaware of the damage.

The clean up would cost a fortune and take months if not years and in any case building for habitation would never be permitted for many years beyond that.

"Now William your report is private, I don't....."

William interrupted "Of course it's awful no one will know from me, let sleeping dogs lie I say"

"Was William fishing for something or just naïve?" Toby thought "He jumped in too quick there, he's no fool though. He must know what is at stake."

William just smiled in anticipation; they both knew what was going on here.

"You have been very helpful William I think a bonus of five thousand pounds would be in order don't you?"

William continued to smile but didn't answer. Toby understood the silent negotiation.

"In view of your considerable risk I think that perhaps a little more would be better."

They settled on eight thousand to be paid in cash. William handed over the files told Toby that he had already deleted the company files anticipating the need for discression and the probable outcome of this meeting. They parted with William on his way to a much-needed holiday, all records of his ever having met Toby or W.W. erased for good. William Rose was unlikely to keep any records, as that would be just as incriminating for him as for Toby. He was pretty confident that Bill Rose would do as he said but Toby would task his PI to check this out; make sure he had gone away as promised; perhaps search his home and office for any forgotten paper or digital trail. No loose ends; they come back and bite.

Nosey Miss Fairchild had stumbled on his money transfers during another investigation. She had followed this up and found the sales of W.W. property were unusual for a successful company and was wondering why move the money. This led to her discovering the land purchase and the pending sale to a European Consortium. She did not know about the survey, no one did except Toby, Sandra and the long gone surveyor. If she started to ask questions about the history of the land or raised doubts in the minds of the intended purchasers the whole deal could collapse.

Toby had her followed. The private investigator installed bugs on her phone and computer. Although he could not get into her encrypted data he had built up a picture of her worrying interference. Toby was afraid that with her skills she would discover the PI's presence and have her suspicions confirmed, so called him off after this initial report.

The Euro group would take ages to draw up plans and apply for permissions. Surveys would be instigated of course but were six months away. The pollution would eventually be discovered, when questioned he would of course feign surprise and sorrow, but by then the money and if necessary he too would be long gone.

He didn't know his 'Euro Brothers' very well but suspected they would be unforgiving in their retribution. He needed an escape route or even better a scapegoat. He did not know which would serve him best, but had an inkling.

Chapter 12

He had covered his tracks well enough. For sure they would think it was just an accident. She might or might not recover, it didn't matter, she would remember nothing significant and even if they find out who she is, despite his mistakes at the time there was no way it would lead back to him. He was being paid well and now was the time to collect, lie low and anticipate enjoying the fruits of his labour.

He sat on the park bench as arranged waiting for her to arrive. He didn't like the idea of being back in Basingstoke but she said they should not be seen together in London. She argued they were also able to take the train to Portsmouth easily from there and catch the night ferry to be in France by the morning and then by hire car to Spain. Debating with himself why they should go to Spain and not stay in England somewhere quiet when his thoughts drifted back to when he had first met this woman who was to become his benefactor and he her lover.

He had been tired cold and feeling sorry for himself making his way from platform three waiting room to the café on platform one. His train had just been cancelled which meant almost an hour wait for the next. He was leaving Basingstoke to try and find work in London. Running away from his job as a car salesman having been caught giving 'discounts' to other dealers for a consideration. It had been good while it lasted but had to leave before his employer decided to teach him the kind of lesson he probably deserved but did not relish.

A hot coffee and a pie would help warm him and pass the time before the next train.

She was sitting alone in the far table adjacent to the counter. The café was narrow with several customers supping and munching sitting at various tables. The contrast in temperature hit him as he entered, almost uncomfortably warm and humid, he shivered and felt hot at the same time. He moved to the counter with just one guy in front of him who was paying for his tea and sandwich. 'Coffee with milk please, err and a sausage roll' He said "Do want that hot or cold luv" She asked "Um, cold is ok ta" He paid, took his cup and plate and looked around without luck for a vacant table.

"Do you mind if I sit here" as hers was the nearest and best vacant place.

"Fine" was her curt reply eyeing him from head to toe.

He felt uncomfortable under her scrutiny but sat down anyway. "My darn trains been cancelled, is yours ok?" He asked trying to be pleasant and ease the tension that seemed to be present.

"No, mine was the cancelled one for London, I presume that was your train too" she followed consulting her watch "we have half an hour or so to wait I think"

"At least it is warm in here" he offered keeping the small talk alive.

"Mmm" was all she muttered. Silence followed. He sipped his coffee and sampled the cold sausage roll now wishing he asked for it to be heated. "Are you from round here?" She said.

"Err, yes and no, I've been working here for a few months but am moving back to London for a new job" He did not wish to elaborate on his precarious situation.

"What's that then?"

"Oh, I'm in the motor trade" again not wanting to volunteer too much.

"Good for you. I know nothing about cars; I usually use trains and taxis. I think with living in London a car would be more trouble than it was worth" was her reply.

"You are probably right, but I'm glad not everyone thinks like that or I would be out of business"

A polite half laugh from both. The conversation continued with small talk, her asking and him replying until she said

"I think our train will be in soon, I'm going to cross over to the other platform. Join me if you like, it will be nice to have company on the train."

"Sure, that would be fine by me" He replied stuffing the remains of his inedible sausage roll into his empty cup.

At just under six feet she stood tall even in her brown flat-heeled boots.

Sandra wore navy trousers, with a knee length charcoal smock and a grey overcoat covering her slim figure. Not young, maybe thirty six or so she had thick dark high-lighted hair well styled in a kind of plaited bun, small silver drop earrings set off a tanned face immaculate make up and glossy red lipstick. Well spoken with a southern accent, not posh, but with a softness that could be seductive. Her disarming smile showed perfect white teeth.

They boarded the train together and before they reached London he had told her his sorry tale. She had listened sympathetically and offered to take him to a friend who would provide him with a room and possibly some work. She had totally taken him in and soon he would be ready to do her bidding.

They arrived at Victoria Station, left the crowded train and moved en masse along the platform to the exit gates. She was behind him as he pushed his ticket in the barrier slot passed through quickly and away to be clear of the bustling passengers, turned and waited for her to exit. She held back a little letting some of those hurrying go by in front thinking, "Do I stay with this guy or give him the slip" She made the decision, moved through the barrier towards where he was waiting.

"What do we do now?" he said all thoughts of his original plans gone from his mind.

"We'll get a taxi to my place first then I'll call my friend to find you somewhere to stay"

"Are you sure?" remembering his earlier intensions "I have a mate in Vauxhall who will put me up till I find somewhere so there's no need to trouble you really." He was glad when she insisted

"Come on it's no problem, in any case I may have a job for you so I don't want you too far away"

If she had been by herself she would have taken the tube but wanted to be alone with him. It took a while to cross London; she sat close to him in the cab, much closer than necessary in the generous rear seat.

He felt her legs touching his making him feel warm inside. He hadn't been close to a woman for a long time now, not since splitting with Joan, almost two years now. She reached out took his hand.

"You and I are going to get along just fine." She whispered, gently squeezing his fingers and resting her head on his shoulder. He didn't move, his body was buzzing with anticipation, not wanting it to end. His luck had changed he could feel it in his bones.

Sandra's apartment on the top floor of a converted factory building in the heart of Shoreditch was modern not as luxurious as some but better than anything the man had seen before. Toby had acquired many buildings in this area. Some had been demolished and replaced with towers of offices, some that had some history were listed so had been converted into high quality dwellings and either sold or rented out. Sandra's was a perk as part of her job. City of London accommodation was limited, a bustling metropolis during weekdays, with its myriad of financial workers, but almost deserted other times.

"Help yourself to a drink in the cabinet there, or a coffee if you want, have a look round you'll find what you want.. I'm going to have a shower and change..won't be long." She disappeared from view leaving the door open to what must be her bedroom.

He stood mesmerized, taking in the huge open plan room with its stainless steel kitchen to one end, the rosewood dining table and chairs to the side and a magnificent white leather sofa occupying almost the length of a large window. It seemed that the whole wall was glass overlooking the smaller buildings interrupted by the many looming tower blocks. He was transfixed for a full minute before the sound of running water shook him into movement. He imagined her naked in the shower. "Wishful thinking eh?" Noseying in the grand American style fridge he found some small French beers. He helped himself to one, luckily it had a twist off top so didn't have too look for an opener in the multitude of kitchen drawers. He put the cap on the counter and moved to the window supping as he went.

His mind in a whirl "What does she see in me?" He let that thought rest, sat on the sofa sipping his beer. "Whatever?"

Sandra emerged from the bedroom in a light loose slacks and a T-shirt. "I see you found a drink ok, are you hungry?, I can rustle up an omelet or something if you like" "Err.. no I'm fine for the minute... I was wondering about your friend .. you know the one you said with a place for me to kip for a few days."

"Don't fret Gerry we can do that later...relax. If it comes to it you can stay here for a while I have a spare room and I'm out most days anyway. It'll give you time to work out what you want to do. I'll put some feelers out and see what I can find."

Sandra went into the kitchen and emerged with two large glasses of white wine a broad smile across her face.

"I hope you drink wine Gerry, I want us to toast to our chance meeting and a some good times to come."

Gerry smiled back at her not knowing what to say, he was a little bemused "Err.. Fine" he muttered thinking "what does this sophisticated and obviously loaded woman see in me. I'm just an ordinary bloke down on his luck and she's treating me like I was Prince Charming or something" Not one to say no to an opportunity he took the proffered glass and raised it saying "Cheers Sandra, here's to us and big thanks to my lovely hostess for saving me from my mates lumpy put-u-up"

"You are most welcome kind sir" she said mimicking his posture and put on posh voice.

"You know I took to you almost straight away; there's something about you that excites me a bit.

"Perhaps you like a bit of rough?" Gerry responded regretting the words as soon as he said them. "I'm sorry that didn't come out as I wanted.....it's just that you are well spoken and obviously well off and I'm just an ordinary bloke....I didn't mean anything by it "

She moved over and sat very close to him. "Shush.. don't say anything else I understand.'" Her arm snaked slid slowly behind his neck as she kissed him behind his ear. She moved round to his lips and their tongues intertwined for just a second. The sensation in him was electric but before he could react she pulled away and walked into the bedroom leaving him rooted to the couch. She glanced back at him with a knowing smile as she disappeared. The invitation was irresistible.

Chapter 13

"What do you think sir" Mike asked of Mr. Lawson having handed him the blood work and scan.

The consultant surgeon Simon Lawson studied them for a few minutes occasionally looking at the girl.

"There is a mix of barbiturates here that should never be together. Levels that must have been much higher at the earlier time of time of the accident. Lets take another blood now and a urine sample too so we can see how quickly she is dispersing this nasty stuff."

"Yes sir, but how does one survive such a cocktail; the combination of drugs is crazy. The anesthetics are usually used for surgery; she shows no sign of that. Her scan shows no brain damage or tumors or bleeds, and there is no indication of surgery anywhere else. Only some small bruises to her thigh muscles are the only abnormalities I can find."

"I agree. It is something I've never seen before, but it does give a good reason for her condition. I doubt if it self inflicted, to inject this and remain conscious during the process would be impossible."

Mike now had a course of action in mind.

"I'll raise her fluid intake to help flush out the remains of this poison. Maybe some gentle physio to mobilise her arms and legs, it may stimulate some response, what do you think?"

"A good idea Mike but be very careful with the exercises, and keep a close eye on her stats. I'll come by later"

Mike adjusted the girl's drip arranged for another blood sample, asked the nurses to collect a urine sample from her catheter bag. He explained what he was hoping for with the increased fluid and also what he wanted with regard to exercises.

"Keep a close eye on her every twenty minutes at first. If you see any changes in her no matter how small call me at once."

Before he left he moved over to her bed and whispered to her again

"Sleep on sweet girl we will have you back with us soon"

' I have been sleeping too long. I must get up now...help me please I know you are there....Harriet is here waiting...it is time'

Chapter 14

Sandra was well briefed by Toby all she needed was someone she could trust to help with the girl. Gerry was ideal. She had met him by chance when she was in Basingstoke studying the lie of the land. She had already organised the dumping of the truck in the old, and little used, Alton road at the appropriate time and through Toby had acquired the golf with its altered number plate from the same source. Now locked away in the Shoreditch garage. Those guys were seasoned car choppers who owed Toby big time. No way would they supply traceable vehicles. Everything was in place. Next step take the girl. They needed her out of the way for two weeks then the deal would be complete. They could not afford to just kill her, as that investigation would open up a whole can of worms best left asleep. A complicated plan that would secrete her away for the time needed and maybe forever if things went well.

"Now for Gerry" she thought. He was at her apartment, probably asleep or watching TV for he was a lazy bugger. She would put the proposal to him later today after a few glasses of wine and a nice dinner. Money talks with him. He would do her bidding for sure.

Gerry followed Harriet from her office on Malborough road to her flat in Squires Muse a small private road only ten minutes walk away. He found she was a creature of habit, last to leave always at the same time give or take a few minutes and used the same route home without fail. Her flat had a shared entrance with a pair of swing doors that led to a small lobby with a lift. Her flat was on the third floor of ten with two apartments per floor. From his position across the street he could see clearly into the lobby. Harriet always climbed the stairs.

"Must be a fitness nut" he thought "I'm buggered if I'd climb stairs after a days graft if there was a perfectly good lift there" He'd kept the surveillance going on the Wednesday and Thursday; her routine never changed.

On the chosen Friday evening just before dusk Gerry parked the grey unmarked van he'd been given in the parking spot that he'd observed was seldom occupied just a few yards from her doorway.

He waited till five minutes before the appropriate time, left the van and entered the lobby. Sandra was already standing by the lift. He hadn't seen her arrive, she'd walked Harriet's route some ten minutes earlier and arrived ahead of Gerry.

Gerry peered through the side window till he saw Harriet turn the corner of her street. Sandra had opened the lift doors keeping them open with her hand across the safety beam. Gerry lay down on the floor of the lift with his feet protruding into the lobby just a few seconds before Harriet appeared.

"Oh dear...Oh dear" Sandra cried out in a panic stricken voice. "Please help, this poor man just collapsed...I don't know what to do"

Harriet immediately stepped passed Sandra knelt down over the prostrate Gerry. Calmly Sandra removed the loaded syringe from her pocket and plunged it into Harriet's exposed calf. At the same time Gerry turned and grabbed Harriet in a bear hug and dragged her into the lift; he held her until the drug had taken hold. Harriet called out but such a weak cry no one could have heard. Sandra reached through and pressed the button for the third floor then raced up the stairs as the lift door closed.

Sandra arrived at the lift just as the door opened with Gerry holding Harriet under the arm.

She pulled Harriet's keys from her handbag and opened the door. Gerry humped Harriet out of the lift across the hallway and into the flat. They were inside now safe, the whole episode having taken just a few minutes. Both Sandra and Gerry's' pulse rates had risen with adrenalin pumping round their veins. Gerry's through exertion and Sandra's through the excitement.

"Whew.. she's heavier than I thought" puffed Gerry. The door to the flat opened directly into a large living combined dining room with three doors off. One led to a kitchen another to a bedroom and the third was a utility area and toilet. The bedroom was also exceptionally large with one corner set up as an office with a desk, filing cabinet, laptop computer and printer. An ensuite shower room completed the ensemble.

"Put her on the couch for now, she'll be out for a couple of hours yet. Look in the kitchen I'll do the bedroom...and keep it tidy it must look like she has just gone away."

Sandra set about looking for anything that might be significant in Harriet's investigation of WW and Toby. She carefully went through each file extracted three from the cabinet which were directly related and four others which had some links. She then removed the laptop and several memory sticks she found in the desk drawer. Her passport was there too along with other various documents. She just took the passport. Next to the wardrobes. In the top of one was a large suitcase with a smaller one inside, empty. She extracted the smaller case and selected a few clothes and underwear such that she might take on holiday. The bathroom yielded nothing unusual, Sandra removed some toiletries and toothbrush and threw them along with the clothes into the case.

The laptop, files, memory sticks and handbag followed leaving only the mobile in Sandra's hands ready for the next step.

Gerry came into the room

"Nothing much in the kitchen, no papers or anything like you asked, just a shopping list on the fridge"

"OK..I think we have everything we need in here" holding up the suitcase "you have a look in the lounge…look in any drawers and check the bookshelf there may be something tucked away…I'll finish up here"

Sandra opened up the phone.. it was active ready to use, no password needed. She scanned through the names and numbers of the phone book. Then on the call list and finally the texts. There were a dozen or so people involved with work and four other more personal messages from friends. She looked at these to see how Harriet composed her texts. She then selected those to whom she would send the message.

'hi there, im buggered, tuff munf, need a brake, taking leave, bagged grate deal 2 wks in dubai. off tonite c u wen bak luv Hxxx'

Her informal style was easy to copy. She sent the text to her obvious friends and the same to a couple of work colleagues leaving out the 'luv xxx'

"One more scan of the bedroom, all tidy enough" thought Sandra lifting the moderately heavy suitcase off the bed. She moved back into the lounge. "Anything?"

"No nothing ...can we go now?" said Gerry eager to be away.

At that moment Harriet's phone in Sandra's pocket began to chime and vibrate. They both stopped dead. She extracted the phone careful not to touch the screen in case it answered and after what seem like forever it went to voicemail. Sandra waited a moment, dialed the voicemail number.

"....You have three messages the first message timed at ......" The voice mail recording rattled on with a selection of options. She was only interested in the last message, pressed the various numbers needed to retrieve this and waited with baited breath.

'You crafty old thing going on hols without me..bout time you had a break...anyway enjoy...call me when you get back... hugs and kisses...oh do you want me to feed Horrace...text or email me...I'll come by if you want.. Tarrra'

Sandra turned off the phone looked at Gerry he at her.

"Horrace....Dog...or Cat maybe?" she said moving into the kitchen. No sign of a food bowl or litter tray. She stopped and laughed out loud in relief; on the windowsill a bowl. "Haaa....a bloody goldfish...lets go now...check the hallway and stairs and call the lift if it's still not there" Gerry went out and came back a few moments later

"All clear" They each put an arm round Harriet's upper body under her arms and between them lifted her easily to an upright position, walked her out of the flat and into the lift. Gerry held her against the lift wall whilst Sandra returned to pick up the suitcase, close the door and re-enter the lift. They were fortunate no one was around, it was now nearly dark, and most of the residents had arrived home well before Harriet. They had a story prepared about an office party and too much drink if they happened to meet anyone on the way out. Sandra was glad they didn't need to use it.

They lifted her into the back of the van through the side door and within seconds were on their way.

Chapter15

The sub-basement room two floors down in the old Shoreditch warehouse had been well prepared. It was big enough to hold a bed, two largish arm chairs, a fridge, and a kitchen table with a kettle some mugs and utensils. There were also a chemical toilet with a side table on which stood an old-fashioned washbowl and jug. An oil filled electric heater stood in the corner, which made it a little near to comfortable. There were no windows and just the one door. No one can see, no one will hear.

Sandra and Gerry had driven the van into the loading bay. They carried Harriet into the old iron gated lift, which rattled down to the basement then down a narrow stone staircase to the lower floor.

She had been placed on the bed; her outer clothes removed then had been redressed in a loose dressing gown with her legs and arms bound with tape over a soft cloth to prevent chaffing. Sandra made sure Harriet would stay asleep with another shot from the syringe this time in her thigh. Gerry folded her clothes and placed them on the armchair.

“That’s good Gerry. You can take the van back to the lads now and collect the car they give you and bring it back here. Check that it has a full tank, if not fill it up ...pay cash..... They will give you a forged insurance certificate and drivers license of the real owner but with your photo, the number plate is from a real car with a current tax disc and MOT. Learn the number and owners details; in the unlikely event you are stopped you’ll be covered.”

“What will you do will you be ok ?”

“I’ll be alright here, don’t worry about me. I’ll see you in a couple of hours or so. I need to stay with her until it’s time for the move, just you be careful love ok”

With that Gerry left the room climbed the stairs all they way to the ground floor by-passing the old lift, he didn’t trust it to keep working. He opened the automatic roller door of the loading bay, drove the van out into the night, looking in his mirror to see the door roll back down behind him a few seconds after he had left.

Sandra sat in the armchair looking at Harriet with different eyes now that Gerry had gone. Resting on her lap the valise, which contained the drug cocktail she had prepared along with the syringes for their delivery. She stroked the lid imagining the effects she would soon witness. An experiment designed to destroy the mind and leave the body undamaged.

She had studied many books on the use of anesthetics stimulants and hullucogens and even experimented on her own mind with dramatic results at times. She did not know the exact doses required but relished the coming hours when she would find out.

The first dose was a small stimulant to bring her round slowly.

'What is this I can't hold my head up what am I doing here what is this place.'

Harriet had no idea what had happened she was soon to be half way between death and hell but didn't know it. Next a little dose of 'Garin' a fast acting hullucogen.

'why is the green grass pink keep the cat away I don't like them....I'm drowning...I need air...air...air I'm on fire........'

Harriet let out a deep moan which grew into a scream. The nightmare had begun.

Sandra sat entranced excited by the almost instant effect of the drug, "this is going to be fun"

Another shot of anesthetic. Harriet calmed down after a few minutes and fell unconscious again. "Lets try again my sweet, a little different this time" Now the mixture was more adventurous, the needle slowly squeezed the noxious liquid into her thigh.

The blackness became grey then red; her arms grew longer her legs fell to the floor she tried to pick up her legs with her new long arms but couldn't move.

'What is happening to me?'

The ache in her head grew strong then stronger until her eyes were sticking out of their sockets blood was running down her face now she started to scream the fat worm was screwing into her brain. It was going to eat her mind.

'Stop.stop...stop...ooooh please stop the pain...keep the worm away'

Another drop of sleepy stuff. Sandra was enjoying this "let's see what's next my dear"

Sandra proceeded with her cocktails of madness for a full hour with ever increasing horror for Harriet. Sandra then stopped to let Harriet sleep. Harriet was soaked in sweat She was fearful that her subject might die if she continued; she also wanted to see the result of her experiments when Harriet eventually woke.

After an hour Harriet stirred. Sandra lifted her by the shoulders and made her drink some water from a plastic bottle. She coughed and spluttered but some water managed to find its intended passage.

"Hello young lady who are you what is your name?"

"Where am I.... who ....what.......I....I......name ....name....no name...my head hurts......"

Harriet slipped back to her ugly dreams. The worm was still there chewing away.

'.... get out.... get out you filthy thing you are not to be here it's mine.'

Her arms and legs were frozen she could not run or stop this evil beast that was destroying her mind. Self-preservation shut her down to protect her sanity and her soul. She was safe in her shell for now.

'I won't...won't come out till it's gone.'

"I'll let you rest for now" Sandra sat back and closed her eyes. Harriet had almost certainly succumbed to the evil mixture swirling round her brain. Memories will be destroyed or so distorted that the truth will have deserted her. She must be sure though, another half hour will see her recover enough to interrogate what is hoped will be a fractured mind.

'I am here... I will not go.... I will be here.... you will not take me.'

Chapter 16

Sandra Cooper was severely damaged. A woman of independent means, through a substantial inheritance from her parents, her aunt Joan and her uncle Robin was a ruined soul at a very early age.

Robin Cooper, the elder brother of her father, had taken on the care of Sandra when she was just seven. Her mother had died of sepsis due to a riding accident resulting in a broken leg and two broken arms which never healed properly and became infected. Although she cared for her Mother she had accepted her death as God's will but loved her Daddy much more and could never understand why he left her with aunty Joan when all she wanted was to be with him now that Mummy had gone to heaven.

He was unable to cope after his wife had died; Norman Cooper took to drinking and had long periods of utter despair. He never once visited Sandra and eventually overdosed on a mixture of painkillers and Vodka.

Sandra was taken to his funeral but being only eight years old paid no mind to the eulogy extolling the virtues of her late father. She didn't cry, she didn't feel anything much, just a creeping resentment that her World had been taken. Even at that tender age she vowed never to love again, it hurt too much. Her parents had left everything to Sandra in trust with Joan and Robin as trustees.

At eighteen Sandra had been able to access some of the money left by her parents, the rest would come when she was twenty-one. Joan and Robin had cared for her well but although very fond of her had not been able to break down the barrier that had been erected from when she first came to them. Her cousin James, the Cooper's only son was six years her senior, was hardly part of her life. He treated her like a sister when they were together but the age difference and the fact that he was either away at boarding school or university made for an on off relationship which never really had a chance of growing. She did like him and enjoyed being with him at home but would not allow any feelings of affection to grow; if she had let him into her life things might have been different.

By the time she was sixteen all was lost, she was a heartless soul. She had gone to good schools and they expected her to go to university. Sandra had different ideas.

She approached her carers with a carefully thought out plan. She explained that she would dearly love to go to university to study history but also wanted to see some of the World and travel a bit before then. A year in Europe, taking in the culture of different Countries could only be good for her and make her later university studies more relevant. She was very persuasive and they gave in to her request reluctantly.

There were to be rules to ensure her safety of course such as a planned intinery of places to be visited or avoided. Which hostels and hotels to be used. More serious was that she could not be alone she must have a friend to go with or it would not happen.

Three months later she was gone; alone.

Toby came into her life when she applied for a job at WW Enterprises.

Sandra completed her 'grand tour' indulging in every vice not succuming to their addictive power however, returning after one year away to complete her education at university. She was offered a place at London but that would have meant staying with her aunt and uncle so opted for Manchester with the excuse to her adoptive family that it was a much better course. She graduated in history with a two/one achieved with the minimum of academic effort.

Her application at W.W. was for the post of personal assitant to a senior executive. At her first meeting, with the personnel officer, she was relaxed and convincing in her answers where her manner and confidence led to a second interview.

At this interview Toby was present, along with others, silent but watchful. Although no words were exchanged, eye contact being the only communication between them created a certain atmosphere that they alone felt. She responded to the questions from the others automatically providing the standard expected replies but hardly able to avert her eyes from Toby's gaze. She did not realise at the time that Toby was the executive in question but left thinking she had failed leaving with a "We will let you know" ringing in her ears.

Two days later she received a phone call to come to the office for a final interview. This turned out to not be an interview atall but the job offer itself. From that day on Sandra was Toby's main confidant and he her mentor.

Toby immediately worked on Sandra, moulding her to his way of thinking. Giving her difficult tasks to test her. She never failed him. There was a joining of like minds that was more than Toby could put his finger on. Sandra's desire for danger enabled him to take chances that he would have avoided on his own.

He loved her but not in a sensual way for he was dormant as a man. It did not worry him unduly for he had no idea what it was that other men felt when close to a woman but in the presence of Sandra he felt he had met a spirit of his kind. The fact is that Sandra's mild psychotic tendencies were probably the main reason for his being so attracted to her. He never trusted Sandra not knowing why but self preservation made him cautious and although he loved her, he loved himself more.

For Sandra Toby was her hero, he took her to extremes in the cut-throat world of business she never would have known, it fed her need to be ruthless nurturing her psychosis to its terrible and deadly conclusion.
Little did Toby realise what a monster he was helping to create.

Chapter17

Gerry had gone over it in his mind so many times he felt he could do it blindfold. Harriet was supported by the seatbelt apparently 'asleep' in the passenger seat; the journey from the warehouse in Shoreditch to Basingstoke in Hampshire would take some time. There would be no problem as they looked just like any other couple driving along. He would be courteous, careful and stick to the speed limits, no silly mishaps.

He knew the area well and had surveyed the selected stretch of road carefully. Since the new dual carriageway was opened the old Alton road was hardly used, just a few locals. There were no CCTV cameras nearby. Early afternoon was best; he had watched several times and on most occasions had not seen a single car.

He drove to a small layby within a mile of where the abandoned truck was parked. He was early so waited for the planned time to arrive. He was grateful for his patience as a car passed by in the opposite direction whilst he was waiting "Good job I didn't jump the gun" he thought "All clear let's do it now"

He drove towards the truck, his hand sweating in the plastic gloves, a quickening pulse pounding in his temples, slowing down considerably at the approach. At the last minute he pulled in clear of the warning triangle and rammed the back of the truck at little more than a fast walking pace.

"Bang…Hissss…Bang….Hisss" "Shit …shit….what the fu…"

He wasn't expecting that. The jolt was much bigger than he anticipated; the airbags had deployed trapping him firmly in his seat. He wasn't hurt just shocked. It took him a second or two to recover then push the now deflating airbag out of his way; instinctively he reached forward to turn off the ignition not noticing that the engine had stalled on impact.

He looked around his mind racing. "Stay calm…all quiet outside and she's not moved, press on"

His heart was pounding harder and faster his head hurt with each pulse. He was re-enacting each stage of the plan in his mind. Next he had to collect the bike before he moved the girl over to the driver's side. He opened the door got out and hurried down the road to where they had hidden the motorbike behind a hedge the day before. He put on the crash helmet and leather gloves, kicked over the engine and rode the few dozen yards back to the car. Now if anyone were to come by it would look as if he had just stopped to help. He removed his helmet and outer gloves parked up and went to the passenger door ready to lift the girl over.

"What the hell.... fu...ing door"

He pulled at the door it was locked or jammed shut. He quickly moved back to the driver's door.

"No No No.. not again..." Panic seize him, this damn door was shut tight too. His head felt like it would burst.

"Bugger! Bugger! ...why does everything go wrong for me... what do I do now?"

He stood there looking at her through the glass, all thoughts of the carefully scripted plan gone. Gerry realised he could do nothing.

Unknown to him the car jackers had replaced the ignition lock that they had smashed during the theft. However the central locking security code did not match the new key. A soon as he switched off the ignition, opened and closed the driver's door; the auto locking mechanism was triggered. Ninety seconds later all doors were locked. It is only muted if the key with the correct code is in or near the car or another door is opened. A safety feature for those of us who walk away from our cars forgetting to lock them. A fatal feature for Gerry and his well rehearsed plan.

"It's not my fault. Bloody air bags.. how the hell did I know they were going to blow and the fuc...ing doors ..what was that all about?"

He knew the plan had gone to ratshit, well almost. At least the girl will be out of the way for some time and won't remember much anyway. He consoled himself with that thought but didn't relish the task of having to tell Sandra what had happened.

Although the road was empty a car could come at any moment and catch him standing there. Gerry had no options left; he had to get out of there now. He re-fitted the helmet, put on his gloves, started the motorbike and headed off back the direction he came.

"Whew !.... lucky me...just in time" he thought as few minutes later a car passed him in the opposite direction. "They will be upon her any moment now they're bound to stop"

With that in his mind he put his aching head down low and accelerated away.

"What the hell do you mean you couldn't move her....she weighs sod- all" Sandra held her breath a moment realising nothing would be achieved by shouting. She wanted a detailed account from Gerry and upsetting him more than he was already would jeopardise that. She wanted to see what damage had been done to their carefully crafted plan.

Sandra listened quietly whilst Gerry explained what had happened; she didn't interrupt but studied him to see if he was leaving anything out or bending the truth. He had 'tells' when he lied, mostly he would put his head to the left side and lift his shoulder when being evasive or being economical with the truth. No sign of that today. He was distressed but in her heart she felt a little sorry for him, as no one could have foreseen his problems. He had coped well enough with a bad situation.

Despite her plan having gone wrong, Sandra decided all was not lost. Most likely whoever found her would remove her from the 'wreck' without a thought about her being in the passenger seat. Even so neither the girl nor the car would be identified for ages, which was the whole idea. She wouldn't tell Toby about the fuck up though, just in case, he could be an unforgiving bastard at times.

Chapter 18

"We must remove all trace of our involvement with this girl, and that includes your Gerry." Toby was adamant that he was a liability they could ill afford.

"I can pay him off' Sandra offered with enough to leave the Country"

"Not good enough Sandra, he'll get caught doing something stupid and won't keep his mouth shut. He is a threat to us alive you must get rid now"

She liked having Gerry around and wanted to have him available for later when all their problems were over. However deep down she agreed, he was a weak man who would crumble under pressure. She couldn't keep him and have Toby too. He had to go. Her mind was racing now

"How, where..not here in London eh?"

"No not here. You still have to pay him don't you. Arrange to meet him somewhere in Basingstoke. Make some excuse to get him there after all it's where he came from and it will keep any enquiries local."

She nodded her agreement.

"That's good; yes he has enemies there which will confuse the police if they get involved. He won't want to go back there though, I will have to find a good reason" She started to form a plan.

Sandra thought back to how she had tranquilized Harriet and despite Toby instructing her to destroy everything in that room she had kept the drugs and needles in her flat. She knew that a full dose of Midaziolam would trigger a heart attack and mixed with diazepam would be quick and painless.

She ran her idea by Toby, not mentioning that she still had the drugs. Toby, knowing how ruthless she could be said.

"I leave it to you my love your plan should work fine just be mindful of CCTV and wear gloves"

She smiled at him, turned and almost skipped out excited by her quest.

Toby thought "Cold heart that one I must be very careful, another loose end that may have to be dealt with."

Chapter 19

Detective Chief Inspector Craig Bean, whom everyone called 'Beanpole' since a lad because he was six feet two and skinny as a rake. He had always been thin and no matter how much he ate or drank, and he did like a drink, he never gained an ounce. Craig was diligent and thorough in his investigations, understanding the need to ensure evidence was solid and uncompromised. He had learnt early in his career that prosecutions would fail for sure if procedures had been slack. The CPS was his master in that. Weeks pursuing villains would come to nothing, even if the evidence were overwhelming when some inexperienced or over enthusiastic copper cut corners. He had seen guilty men walk free too often to ignore the rules now.

He had been a DI for many years his promotion to Chief came about through time served and through his old boss being promoted to Superintendent. Promotions in the police were slow in coming and were often politically motivated especially the higher ranks, not so much at his level or in rural districts. Competition for the top spots in areas like London was fierce.

His promotion did not change things too much he tried to be as active in the field as before. The downside was the extra administration and financial responsibility kept him behind the desk for which the pay rise did little to compensate.

Craig didn't sleep much and liked to keep ahead of his team so all reports were sent to his e-mail. He checked them regularly and became aware of the case of the young girl whilst reading Andrew's initial report among his e-mails. It seemed to be routine at this stage but some instinct told him to keep a close watch, in fact there were some changes about to take place in the Basingstoke nick; he would call a meeting first thing with Fred, Peter and all the others.

Craig Bean walked into the crowded squad room followed by a medium height dark skinned woman in a navy suit. No one took much notice at first, it was busy with almost all the officers of the station either sitting or standing and chatting in groups all waiting for the Chief to arrive.

"Right everyone is here I think...a bit of hush please" said Craig with his voice raised over the voluminous background level.

'"Settle down now...." The level fell and every one turned to see the Chief and a middle aged lady at the door, moving towards the end of the room. "Thank you all for coming I know some of you have lots to do and are eager to get on with it so I won't keep you very long. I want to introduce you to DI Toni Webb. She is joining us, not before time I might add, from Southampton to replace DI Eddie Black who as you all know retired last year."

Toni stepped forward and nodded to the assembly who were mumbling their 'hellos' and nodding back.

"She will be working with Sergeant Mann and Constable Andrews" pointing at both men in turn. "Welcome Toni.... Now those of you who are not directly connected to the current accident or other CID investigations can leave if you have other things to do. Remember all of you there is something not very good going on in our patch, so keep your eyes and ears open; report anything and I mean anything out of the ordinary to either Sergeant Mann or DI Webb."

The room cleared leaving both CID teams, some of the technicians and station officers.

"Right Fred where are we with the girl in the car?"

"I phoned the hospital, no change in her condition, there seems to be no physical damage. Still waiting on blood and other tests, they will call me when they know more. The car and truck are now with the accident investigators at Alton, Henry will know more soon, however he did say his initial thought are this was no normal accident"

"What about ID?"

Peter Andrews then explained about the locked doors and the number plate ringing and that he was no further forward in finding out the girls name.

"There are no persons matching her description reported missing either locally and the Southern Counties or the Met. I'll check again later today maybe she hasn't been missed yet"

"Good Peter keep onto that and let me know one way or another. Fred get onto Henry, the car is our only lead at the moment whilst the girl is out and unidentified. Constable Masters please arrange for the witnesses to come to the station I want to talk to them"

He turned to DI Colin Dale the leader of the other CID team at Basingstoke. "Give me a minute Colin I'll be with you soon"

He now turned back to Toni Webb.

"Toni this is Fred Mann and the young man over there is Peter Andrews they are your new team. Fred is an old hand here and will get you up to speed both with the case and the others at this station. Ask him what you like he will almost certainly have an answer."

He turned back to Colin and his guys who had been patiently waiting.

"Now Colin thanks for waiting, where are we with these spate of burglaries?"

"We are close sir, we have prints from the last job that match to a Marius Welbrooke who has form for breaking and entering. He did six months on IOW and was released six weeks ago just about the time these break-ins started. We have an APB out. We are checking his old haunts and mates. Informants say he has been seen around and will give us the nod, no address that has panned out yet but we should have him soon."

"Good ...good keep on that for now we may need your help if this other thing escalates as I think it might."

Craig then introduced Toni

"This is DI Colin Dale, his number two here is DS Jonny Musgrove and this is DC Mel Frazer." They all expressed their welcomes and shook hands awkwardly before leaving.

Craig moved towards his office Toni followed behind as he passed by Fred and Peter he said "Come to my office before you go"

"This is a new team and I think it will be a good one too. DI Toni Webb comes to us with an excellent record, Fred here has a wealth of experience and young Peter is technically aware and has a good nose. It may take a while for you to settle, I want you to work at it, I need you to be up to the mark damn quick. Anyway I did not bring you in here for a pep talk but to tell you that Peter Andrews promotion to Detective Constable has deservedly come through. Well done Peter"

He then passed him his new warrant card.

"you can ditch the uniform at last"

The words Peter had longed to hear; he was not too surprised but even so was more than pleased. He had passed all the exams and had worked his arse off for the last year.

"Thank you Sir, I'll not let you down"

"I know... I know, now off you all go and keep me informed of any developments.

Chapter 20

She had not killed before, although there were persons she would like to have dispatched without doubt, she just didn't have the nerve. Wondering if she would have the nerve now made her more and more tense as the time approached. She felt the adrenaline surge and her icy heart beat faster. "Concentrate...concentrate. Just do as planned and you'll be fine" she urged herself.

Having made a survey of the park earlier she knew it was usually quiet at this time of day with only a dog walker or two who were unlikely to be anywhere near the chosen bench. Toby had identified any CCTV in the area and she was aware how to position herself so as to be undetected. She waited by the gate, wearing a long black coat, hood up and scarf masking her lower face. She peered through the iron mesh of the gate support posts and spotted that the man was sitting on the bench as expected. He was still, as if asleep, but she doubted that. He was sure to be thinking about the money and her too no doubt.

It had been difficult to persuade him to meet her in Basingstoke park.

"I don't see why you can't take me with you to get the money " Gerry almost demanded.

She had risen early and woke him slowly with a back massage which turned into a love session as she knew it would. He was always pliable after sex which is how she needed him to be if he was to do as she asked.

" Because we should not be seen together my boss has someone inside the police who says they are on the look out for a couple with descriptions similar to us"

"How the hell did they do that"

"Some CCTV footage apparently, anyway I want us to leave as soon as we can. We'll cross the Channel by ship it's safer than by air and the best way for us is from Portsmouth on the night ferry. I have already booked a cabin. You can go down to Basingstoke easily from here, I will have to travel half across London to pick up the money there's no point in both of us doing that. I'll get the tickets and meet you there later. I'll give you your money then we can travel the last bit together."

Sandra was making it up as she went along unsure if he would accept her not very convincing explanation.

Gerry mumbled under his breath not understanding why he had to make such a complicated and broken journey. He knew she had a complex mind so it never occurred to him to doubt her sometimes twisted logic. He only ever wanted to please her so convinced himself that going away was what he wanted too. He was weak and she knew it; he did as he always did, agreed to what she asked.

She had checked the hypodermic syringe, several times; in her right hand pocket a piece of cork protecting her gloved fingers from the deadly spike.

No one else was in her view or near her intended approach.

She knew he trusted her, more than that, he was entranced. Sex with him had been a means to an end, pleasant enough as he was, thank God, a considerate lover, however she felt no qualms for what she was about to do. There would be no fear in him, just greed and lust.

He was expecting a really nice pay-off and her promise to meet up with him for their trip to the

Portsmouth Ferry terminal later filled him with anticipation. She would find him at ease and completely unaware of her hideous intentions.

She removed her hood and approached from behind walking on the grass so he would not be aware of her until the last moment. He was startled from his reverie by her sudden words of greeting.

"Hello there" from his rear. He swiveled still seated to see her standing behind him.

"Wow...you mad me jump...I was day dreaming a bit...is everything OK?"

"Of course my love" she replied with her disarming smile making him soar inside. "Here is a little present for you" She dropped the bag with the money on the seat beside him. He immediately turned to look in the bag, he couldn't resist, as she knew he would.

Her heart rate jumped as she eased the cork from the sharp point and as he bent over to examine his prize, exposing his bare neck, she plunged the needle deep into the soft flesh behind his ear. Infusing his blood with the deadly mixture. There was little reaction just an "Ow!.....what are you...."

His hands contracted inside the bag gripping the notes in desperation as the nausea gripped his body and the dizziness overtook him. He was unconscious in seconds and dead soon after, almost unaware of what had happened.

"Its done" Time seemed to stand still for Sandra. "That was easy" she thought "for me as well as him"

Her heart was pounding and her legs started shaking, the excitement and enormity of what she had done was overtaken as the fear of discovery set in. She walked unsteadily round the bench tore the money from his stiff fingers and closed the bag. She sat him up with his head bowed, wiped the small drop of blood from his neck. She then checked his pockets. Sandra removed everything from his wallet except some money, two credit cards and his driver's license. She took his mobile as it probably had calls and texts that could come back to her and replaced it with a pay as you go that she had bought earlier with a couple of local calls made by her to a restaurant and the garage where he used to work. She wanted him found but without a suspicion of foul play. If they did not go along with the heart attack they would at least be searching locally for an answer.

The activity had a calming effect, her legs had stopped shaking. She looked round to see no one near, just a few people walking along the path the other side of the park. She felt relieved, even if they were looking from that distance it would not seem out of the ordinary. She slowly retraced her steps across the grass, resisting the urge to run, exhilaration now coursing through her body. She turned for one last look, spied him from the gate. He was only a man asleep on a park bench. She walked out of the park through the back streets of the nearby housing estate with her hood up head held low. When found they would think it was just a heart attack, in any case there was little to link him to her. The estate was a twenty-minute walk to the Town center. She felt safe now, took down her hood put the scarf in her pocket and strolled jauntily with a fantastic buzz in her head. "Better that sex, yea better than anything" soon she was on a train heading back, on a high all the way to London.

They were safe now Toby would be waiting for her, she had missed being with him so much, keeping Gerry engaged had taken all her time lately. She had chosen well, despite his stupid mistakes. Gerry Grey had removed a major problem and she had removed him with no chance of comeback to her and Toby.

Chapter 21

"There's a body in the park on Southside get over there sergeant and see what it's about" DCI Craig Bean was not in a good mood. "This business with the girl and nicked car is weird. I'm going to call the hospital to see if she's awake yet. I need some answers. Take Andrews with you, if anything is out of place call me and I'll send DI Webb over otherwise deal with what ever needs to be done. I need DI Webb with me for the next hour"

With that the DCI was gone leaving Sergeant Mann open mouthed, with no time for even a 'Yes sir' or to ask any questions. Fred Mann moved downstairs to the front desk "Hey Foggy what's this body in Southpark, who reported it? Is anyone there?"

"Only just came in ten minutes or so ago Fred, some kids found him apparently thought it was a guy asleep, got a bit of a shock I think. Anyway they ran to the park keeper, who called it in, he said he is guarding the corpse till you arrive. Oh..he called an ambulance too, don't know if they are there yet though.... Good luck"

'Ta, ok I'm on my way out there now, call Andrews for me would you and tell him to meet me there" Fred dumped his now cold undrunk tea on the counter and stuffed the half eaten canteen egg sandwich in his pocket, his rumbling stomach cursing him for getting up too late for breakfast. He told his overactive juices to be quiet. He didn't sleep much lately and needed shuteye much more than he did food.

It was only five minutes to the park in the car that he parked, unknown to him, by the very gate used by Sandra. He could see the bench with a cluster of people around. As he got closer he saw to his relief that Constable Andrews was ushering away a group of dog walking onlookers.

"How did you get here so fast Peter?"

"Morning Sarge. I was on my way from the train when Foggy called me. I was right by the top gate only two minutes away. I've checked, there's no pulse he's stone cold, been dead some time, found a wallet with thirty pounds a couple of credit cards and drivers license, a mobile phone too but nothing else. Name of Gerald Grey, aged forty six, address is 16, Alder Close"

The park keeper was standing on the grass behind the bench looking anywhere except at the body. Fred called him to come over to the path away from the corpse.

"Hello sir, I'm Sergeant Mann and this is Detective Constable Andrews, please what is your name and what can you tell me about this?"

"I'm Monty Baker sir. Been here twelve years never had one of these..." pointing at the body "....in all that time, poor chap"

"I'm sorry you have had to witness this but please go on"

"Well I was in my office over by the top gate when the two lads came running in shouting 'there's a dead man come quick'. I thought it was a prank at first but one of the boy's was crying so I wasn't sure. I told them to show me where. The one who was crying did not want to go and ran off. The other lad agreed and we came over here"

"What happened to the boy, did you get his name?"

"Oh.... soon as we got here said he had to find his mate and ran off..." Pointing to the Southgate. "...I couldn't stop him I was a bit taken aback"

"That's alright, not your fault, what next?"

"I used the mobile to call an ambulance and the police who told me to wait here"

"Did you touch the body?"

"Oh no he's just as you found him"

"Did the boys touch him?"

"I doubt it.. but they might have...I don't know"

"Thanks Monty, by the way have you ever seen him before?"

"He wasn't there when I closed last night, I didn't come this way this morning... so no"

"What about other days?"

"Er ...maybe lots of people use this park I'm not sure I don't know"

"Thanks again Monty, you did fine, you can go back to your office now. We may need to speak to you again for a statement. We know where to find you if we do. Oh by the way did you know those boys?" Monty Baker shook his head

"Not really, not their names, although I've seen them in here before I'm sure they are local"

"Ok we'll get a description from you later" Monty did not need to be told twice, he was gone.

The ambulance and paramedics were just then arriving at the bottom gate. One of them, a girl, ran up the hill towards the bench, the other more slowly carrying the heavy medical pack.

"No rush lass he's gone!" called Mann, waving at her to slow down. She carried on anyway arriving a few seconds later very out of breath. She immediately checked for vitals then looked up at Mann

"You never know... " she said panting "...but you are right" She paused a minute waiting for her partner to arrive.

"No sweat Joe he's been dead a while"

He nodded at the officer and said

"I'll have a look anything suspicious sergeant errrr...?"

"Oh I'm Sergeant Mann. No nothing I can see a heart attack maybe, he's a bit young though?"

Jane looked over at the policeman who was maneuvering the inquisitive by-standers away from the scene.

"Oh it's Peter" she exclaimed, she did not recognise him at first as he was out of uniform. Surprised at the coincidence.

"We've met before, the other night a young girl...and an accident. I'm Jane Thornby and this is my oppo. Joe Felix"

Joe nodded at Mann again.

"Hello Jane" said Peter feeling embarrassed but not knowing why. Mann looked at both, raised his eyebrows, but said nothing.

He walked up to Jane.

"This death is not suspicious at the moment so no need to call out the pathologist. He died, apparently alone, earlier today, no witnesses as yet" reminding himself to trace the two boys. He had searched the dead man's pockets and found a wallet with some cash and a couple of cards and a driver's license. A mobile phone and a few coins were the only other items he could find.

"The name's Gerrald Grey, local address from his license, maybe an autopsy will be ordered to determine the nature and time of death. Jane please will you take the body to the morgue. We will inform the Coroner he will decide" Peter looked over to Sergeant Mann and got the nod of approval for this decision.

Jane covered the body with a sheet whilst Joe went to fetch the trolley and body bag from the ambulance. She walked over to Andrew.

"Any news of the girl from yesterday?"

"Not yet, lots of strange things there though. CID is involved now. My Chief is onto something"

He turned away to deal with more passers by.

"Damn nosey buggers ..won't keep away" he said under his breath.

"Move along please nothing to see here"

The gathering group of onlookers reluctantly dispersed with unsavory mutterings Peter ignored.

"Sorry Jane a bit busy here call me and we can meet up if you like"

Just then Joe arrived back, a bit hot and slightly annoyed at having had to push the mobile stretcher up the hill on his own. He did not want to cramp Jane's rare chance to socialise so let it go with a good heart, relishing the opportunity to pull her leg later.

Jane moved off preparing to bag the body and strap it to the trolley. Five minutes and they were ready.

"Ok, you call me" she said as they moved the trolley onto the path and down the hill.

Whilst this was going on Fred was looking on the grass in front of the bench. Some footprints all mixed up in the mud, no clear marks. He walked along the path in both directions, head down, clean enough nothing to see. He moved over to the grass behind the bench again a mix of footprints. Not unexpected with everyone traipsing around. The park keeper the boys and the paramedics and God knows who else. He looked back down the hill. It looked to Fred like someone came this way across the grass it's trodden down, nothing definite no footprints. He spotted a piece of paper in the grass some ten feet away.

"Probably nothing..." he thought

"...just a dirty hanky..but you never know"

He bent down for a closer look, just as he thought a paper handkerchief, he lifted it with a bit of stick he found nearby. It was a small smudge but for sure it looked like blood. Fred put on a pair of plastic gloves and placed it carefully in an evidence bag he always carried in his large inside pocket. He reminded himself to have a word with the Coroner as this small blood speck made him unsure. He decided that it was probably nothing so decided not to cordon off the area as a crime scene but would certainly press the Coroner to order an autopsy just to make sure. He decided to have another look round and to see if there were any CCTV cameras nearby, again his feeling of something not quite right was nagging him to do more.

He called the Chief and voiced his suspicions.

"Thanks Fred I am of the same mind as you, we don't want to escalate this as it's probably a natural death, we'll wait for the Coroner and the Post Mortem result; wrap it up for now, come in and let DI Webb know what has happened."

With no sign of anything going on the clusters of nosey parkers had dispersed.

"All done here Sarge" They walked together down the path towards the lower gate just as it started to rain.

"I have a car here we'll go back together, save you a walk and getting wet Peter."

"Thanks Sarge shall we go directly to his address now, maybe he has someone there waiting for him to come home?"

"No not yet, were only a few minutes from the nick. Lets go and speak to the new DI first, we have plenty of time for that sad task. Perhaps she will want to do that, we shouldn't take too much on without her, don't want to put her back up on the first day do we?"

Ten minutes later the two policemen were climbing the stairs to the squad room. The DCI's office was closed and DI Toni Webb was sitting at her desk. "Hello you two" she stood and walked towards them her hand held out. Fred moved in and shook her hand Peter waved his reply as Toni let go of Fred's hand.

"Lets get aquainted face to face eh? Chief Bean has told me something about you and the set up here. Now put me in the picture about this morning." Fred explained about Gerrald Grey and his doubts.

"No need to make a decision yet we'll treat it as a natural death for now, if your doubts have any foundation we'll soon find out. Let's go to his house in a minute. We can get ahead of this just in case. Constable you send the paper handkerchief and his phone off for analysis. We need a WPC just in case there is a wife at his house, as we need to leave someone there if they become distressed. Sergeant can you organise that, do you have a car?"

"No problem ma'am, I'll be waiting for you outside in five minutes." Fred left straight away leaving Peter behind with the new DI.

"Well done on the promotion lad, nice to have a keen DC; young eyes can always make a good team great, I'm sure we will get on fine. Let me know about the blood, phone and when the autopsy is to take place. Here is my mobile number. I'll see you later"

"Thank you Ma'am, I'll be in touch as soon as I can" With that they both left.

Chapter 22

The nurses had been diligent in following Mike's instructions. Exercising her arms and raising her legs bending them at the knees in gentle rhythmic movements. They lifted her slightly rolling her onto her side for a few minutes and then on to the other, before returning her to lying on her back.

They had increased her fluid intake and emptied her urine from the catheter bag regularly taking timed samples before disposing of the contents.

Her vitals remained little changed a small elevation in BP and a slightly better colour in her cheeks were all. This continued for four hours when during the next exercise period nurse Jacobs felt a little resistance in the arm movement. "Sister ....sister" she called to her colleague "come here I think we have something"

"What is it Jo?"

"I'm not sure.. I felt her holding back though it's gone now, should I call Doctor Smith?"

"Let me see" Sister May Baker stepped forward on the opposite side to Jo and took her other arm. "Lets work together , up...up gently now down slowly...

again… up… up ..” there it was; a push back. “You’re right I felt it then just a little, what about you?”

“No nothing this time” said Jo,

“Leave it there then I’ll call doctor he will want to see this.” With that May returned to her desk and put out a call to Mike Smith whilst Jo adjusted Harriet’s position and bedding.

Mike was having five minutes half dozing in the Doctors office, between ward rounds, when the call came “No peace for the wicked he thought” but he became immediately alert when he saw where the call had originated. He bounded out of the room and along the corridor up the stairs two at a time ignoring the lift. Within two minutes he was beside Harriet’s bed taking in May’s verbal report.

“it was only momentary doctor but we both felt it, thought you should know.

“Yes; sure; fine… I was hoping she had come round”

“You did say report anything no matter how slight”

“Quite right of course I was just hoping… maybe” Mike leant forward and held Harriett’s hand; he squeezed her fingers gently and lifted her arm to vertical; he held it there for a few seconds then let it down slowly.

"Yes yes there it is" the arm did not fall as he let go. He held her hand again lowering the arm feeling the resistive response.

"This is good the first sign of a connection; mind to body. Great news; now May please let me have her urine samples I will take them to the lab myself. Keep up what you have been doing I think we are going to be lucky with this one, I'll be back soon but call me...you know...anything"

Mike collected the box of sample from nurse Jo and marched out of the ward his destination the lab, he wanted these test results a.s.a.p.

Having deposited the samples with the lab tech who was made well aware of the urgency required, Mike returned to the wards thinking 'I'll wait for the results before I call Simon she may even be more responsive by then'

He wasn't the only one on duty but there were dozens of patients on the medical wards all demanding his or some doctors' attention the pressure was relentless. The girl was just one of many under his care he continued his delayed rounds.

'Stop pulling me I'm not ready yet..let go. I try my best to break away but my arms and legs are not working. I am running slowly.... to nowhere.....why am I waving ? there is no one to wave at. I can see the light ..... can I hear voices...no...maybe...yes someone is there. Not the worm....oh God let it be not the worm.'

Jo and May continued in turn with the exercises for ten minutes with a ten-minute break between. There were the occasional resistances to movement but nothing definitive.

After two hours they called Mike with a progress report who told them to rest her for a while and that he would be back on the ward soon.

During the next time Jo checked the catheter bag she noticed her arm had moved from her side and was now lying across her chest. She wasn't sure at first so moved it back to her side and immediately her arm moved back to her chest. "Sister....sister...May!"

"What is it?"

"Call Mike she is moving on her own"

By the time Mike arrived by her bed she had not only moved her arm but had moved her other arm and head.

Her eyes had opened and closed a few times but were now closed. Her whole body had shuffled down as if to make herself more comfortable.

Mike was elated "A real good sign this, at last she is coming out of it" Mike did a full check of her vitals and reflex responses with near normal results.

"Hello pretty lady you are finally coming back to us I see"

Mike whispered once more in Harriet's ear.

"Keep a close watch here Sister. You can reduce the drip back to normal now. I'm going to get the latest blood results and talk to Mr. Larson I won't be long"

'I'm here....I'm here....wait I won't be long.....the soft voice has gone .....come back....wait for me.... the worm has gone it is safe to come out now...so tired.....must sleep...'

Mike was back with the blood results and was glad to see they had returned to near normal.

"Hello there, lay still, you are safe now" He was speaking gently to Harriet as her eyes slowly opened and he came into her blurry view.

"What is this place....where am I?" She spoke aloud for the first time since she knew not when, surprised by her own voice. She blinked a few times to clear her vision and tried to sit up.

"Hello young lady, at last you are with us. You are in hospital near Basingstoke. You have been involved in an accident and have been unconscious for a while but are safe now and uninjured as far as we can see. I am Doctor Smith just lay still for now as I need to check you over"

Mike proceeded to take her pulse and blood pressure more for her to be assured of where she was than for the readings.

"What is your name? we couldn't find ID when you came in. Is there someone we can contact for you?"

"I'm Mary no.... I'm Harriet..oh I don't know. What is wrong with me?" She was getting agitated.

“Stay calm, no problem, you have had a shock your memory will come back soon……relax” Mike laid his hands on her shoulders easing her back into the pillows. He could see tears in her eyes with her furrowed brow and clenched fists expressing her rising anxiety.

“Shush…shush… its ok…. Relax…..you’ll be fine…close your eyes…rest now.” Mikes soothing voice seeped into her fog bound mind. She slowly settled her tense body and slipped back into a dreamless sleep.

“Mary or Harriet eh?” Mike wondered which “Well anyway some positive response is good” He left her to sleep, with the nurses charged with paging him when she next awoke.

Harriet woke with a start. She looked around and immediately knew where she was but didn’t understand how she got there. There were weird thoughts of monsters trying to eat her brain, she rationalised that this must be the side effect of drugs or something the nurses here had given her. She remembered the doctor’s soothing voice and kind eyes. It struck her suddenly she didn’t know anything about herself, her name nothing! Panic seized her she cried out as if in pain, tears streaming down her cheeks, legs stiff as an overstretched violin string, arms waving violently. "What have you done to me?" she shrieked.

The nurses were unaware that she was awake until they heard her wails of anguish. Immediately they moved to her bedside with intensions of calming her. The panic attack was in full swing.

"Don't touch me" she yelled "Stay away!"

"Call the doctor now" said sister Baker to the nurse Jo. She backed off a little. "Take it easy I won't come any closer, we are here to help you. I'm Sister Baker you have had a bad experience and have been unconscious for some time but are safe now. The doctor is on his way he will explain everything, just try and relax take deep breaths" She smiled at Harriet and continued to talk to her in reassuring tones inducing her to relax and breathe deeply. After a few minutes she calmed and the nurses were able to approach closer.

Harriet was still sobbing sucking in her breath in rapid bursts with less panic and but with a feeling of utter helplessness. "Please help me I am lost"

Mike came into her view "He would help" she knew just by instinct.

"It's all right Sister thank you, I'll stay with her now"

Mike decided to wait a while and let her sleep. He calmed her with soothing words and a gentle massage of her arm. She slept. He waited. Time passed.

Mike saw her eyes flicker as she started to wake. He decided to be bold saying in a confident matter of fact voice.

"Good morning Harriet how are you today?"

"Good morning doctor, I'm fine" Harriet responded without thinking.

"Well then it's about time you were out of that bed so we can send you home soon"

"I...yes...that will be good" she was still half asleep not processing what was being said except in her sub-conscious.

"Where's that then?" he said quickly so as not to break the flow.

" Er...London..Marlborough Road...no..that the office...I don't know..just round the corner...." She stopped to think and broke the spell. " Where did that come from I've no idea?"

Mike seized on the moment.

"There I told you your memory is coming back. Your office is in Marlborough Road now what is your name Harriet or Mary it would be nice to know what to call you?"

"Both I think.... yes I'm Harriet Mary...oh I can't ...I can't remember the rest" She was getting agitated again;

"Take it easy Harriet one step at a time, relax a moment now, more will come soon. Sleep again if you can I'll be back"

Chapter 23

Debbie Taylor woke early that morning. She had a message that an autopsy was required the next day. Suspicious death the Coroner had said. Not totally unusual as there were several cases every year in Hampshire, which were of an indeterminate nature. She had performed too many to count now but only a few suspicious deaths turned out to be through foul play. She did not know it but today was going to be one of those.

Forensic pathology was a path that Debbie had not deliberately chosen but following her initial medical training and some years in St Thomas Hospital as an intern and later as resident and finally senior surgeon specialising in coronary disease. She had been asked by a colleague for advice in a particularly difficult case of a young man who had died from a heart attack with no apparent cause. She became immersed in trying to solve the puzzle eventually tracing it to an allergic reaction to an insect bite. The insect had bitten the man; the inquisitive bug had bitten her restless mind. The next three years were spent in the study of pathology and particularly forensics. Finally she was appointed as a forensic pathologist with the Metropolitan Police.

Debbie was on call to several different authorities this time it was Hampshire Coroners Office. The body had been transferred to her laboratory in Richmond. She arrived at the building to find two detectives waiting for her in the lobby. The receptionist had pointed out Dr. Taylor as she approached the front steps. Toni Webb stepped forward and opened the door for her just as she entered.

"Good morning Doctor, I'm DCI Webb and this is DC Andrews we are here to witness the autopsy of Gerry Grey if that is ok"

"Good morning Detectives" she replied "please follow me, you can wait in the outer office; It will be a little while before I can start so please help yourself to a tea or coffee from the machine over there; my assistant will bring you to the viewing gallery when I'm ready"

"Have you been to an autopsy before?" asked Toni of Peter.

"Once with a group of us as part of training, we didn't see much as we were there near the end and only stayed for ten minutes or so."

"This might be different. if you feel bad don't try and be brave, leave if you need it affects us all at times, right."

"Thanks I think I'll manage"

Ten minutes and two coffees later a young man came and took them along the corridor and up a short flight of steps to the viewing room. The autopsy area had three slabs, a sink, adjacent side tables laid with various tools and unknown pieces of equipment. A white sheet with what they assumed was the body of Gerrald Grey deceased covered the left hand area. The gallery was a mezzanine floor set back about six feet from the front of the tables high enough so they had a good view looking down on the subjects through a long plate glass window. Dr. Taylor entered followed by another person. They were both dressed in green gowns with hats. They had facemasks and protective goggles hanging loose ready for use if needed. The two approached the body. Dr. Taylor looked up at the window and spoke, her voice coming from a hidden speaker such that they could hear every word as if they were in the room

"Ok officers this is Dr. Hart, she will be assisting me in this procedure."

Dr. Hart removed the covering to reveal the naked body.

So it began.

"The subject is a white male of approximately 40 years of age he is a little overweight but appeared to have been in ...."

The autopsy continued for an hour where he had been photographed, finger printed, visually examined all over, opened fully down his front from throat to waist, his organs removed and weighed, his heart examined in detail. Blood extracted, stomach contents collected and all the usual processes of learning the way of demise. Fluids were sent of to the laboratory for analysis. The doctor had commentated on her actions and conclusions to the recorder as well as to the attending detectives. DC Andrews was so engrossed in the processes he managed to overcome his nausea even during the more gruesome carvery, just. They waited until Doctor Taylor had finished and was removing her gloves before they left to descend the stairs. Doctor Hart was left to close the body and return it to the cold storage drawer.

"As I said all the heart muscles had contracted in spasm at once and the muscles of the diaphragm among others had contracted at the same time, this combination does not occur naturally. The heart ceased to pump; death was immediate. Similar results occur with death by electric shock but considering where he was found I suspect some degree of chemical assistance was responsible. We don't know if the drugs were introduce orally or through other means, analysis of the stomach and blood should tell us more however I found a small injection site in the neck which was hardly visible so suspect the latter. If that proves to be the case then you have a third party involved."

"How long before the blood results are ready?" Said Peter jumping the gun, on his new DI, with his question.

"They won't be ready until later today at best but more likely tomorrow depending upon what we find. I'll call you as soon as I know. You'll have somewhere from a suicide to a murder and anything in between to investigate, my thoughts lean towards third party involvement, but don't quote me yet." Before they left she gave them a copy of the provisional report and a copy of his prints.

"Well well, a murder maybe" said Toni as much to herself as to Peter. "Lets get back to the station and see who this guy really was and what he's been up to"

The drive from Richmond back to Basingstoke was conducted mostly in silence with some small talk as befitted their new relationship. Toni was treading quietly for now as she needed the co-operation of Peter and Fred if her future in Hampshire was to be secured. Peter's assuming control at the end of the autopsy, even though a small infringement of protocol was annoying. She would give this DC the benefit of being newly promoted and enthusiastic as her excuse for not pulling him up, however Toni knew she would need to be more assertive with Peter and would start sooner than later. She was unsure of Fred but knew his long service and experience would be more of a help than a hindrance, she would take this slowly until she had become accepted.

As soon as they arrived at the station she tasked Peter.

"Constable Andrews please take the prints and check on this Gerry Grey find out all you can about him. I am going to treat this case as if a homicide for now. We need to get ahead even if it turns out to be something else."

"Yes ma'am right away" Peter was aware of the unspoken situation between them and wanted to return to an acceptable level of seniority.

They climbed the stairs to the squad room, Peter went to his desk and switched on his computer. Toni moved to where Fred was reading some reports. She apprised him of the findings of the autopsy and her intentions.

After just ten minutes at the computer Peter had uncovered some very interesting facts.

"Ma'am you should see this"

"Just tell me" said the DI; she didn't want to leave her desk to look at a computer screen and needed to let Peter know how she expected him to react.

"Gerry Grey has a record, just petty stuff really, drunk and disorderly, resisting arrest, shoplifting just once, he pleaded guilty to that. He never served any time bound over and some community service. This two years ago nothing since. The real enigma here is his print matches the one found on the key fob from the golf concerned with the unknown girl case.'

Toni's attention was instant 'That's a big coincidence, I don't believe in, shame we didn't check his prints earlier, still we weren't to know. Do you have an address and employment details."

"He lives in Chineham and works at a car dealership on the Westwood industrial estate."

"Great, sergeant Mann you get over to his place of work you know what to do. Constable Andrews you and I are going to his house...come on lets go" They both jumped up with a knowing glance at each other. On their way out Toni stopped at the Chiefs office. "You carry on Fred, Peter wait for me in the car."

Toni knocked waited a few seconds and cracked the door of DCI Beans office.

"Come in Toni what is it?" Toni then explained what had been found so far and the significance of the two cases being linked.

"You go and find out what you can from his address, I'll chase up the forensics, hospital and Pathologist. We'll meet back here for a debrief and plan of action this is getting serious."

Chapter 24

Both detectives arrived at the house in Chineham, Gerry's last known address. The modern semi had a small front garden with a low hedge demarking the boundary a short path to the front door, which they approached with trepidation. They were without a WPC so hoped there were no female relatives to console as that was a job she detested. Toni pressed the bell push and waited a few moments later a youth about sixteen answered the door.

"Yes, what do you want, we don't buy stuff from the door?

Toni showed her warrant card. "Good afternoon young man I am Detective Inspector Webb this is Detective constable Andrews is your mother or father in we need to speak to them?"

The lad stood his ground in the doorway "No one's in now they are at work, Mum'll be home any minute what's it about?"

"We are trying to find out about a Mr. Grey, does he live here?"

"Bloody hell what's Gerry done now? The bastard ran off without paying his rent and took me Dad's watch and me Mums' rings and stuff "

"When was that?"

"About three weeks ago I think....oh here's me Mum"

At that point a car pulled up in the drive in front of the garage. A lady climbed out without looking up with two bags of shopping as she walked across the drive she noticed the officers and stopped.

"Who are you what do you want?"

"Don't worry madam we are the police just enquiring about a Mr. Grey. I am DI Webb and this is DC Andrews" again showing his warrant card. As she approached her son came and took her bags.

"They're looking for Gerry Mum" she shook her head

"Oh are they indeed, so are we but he's long gone for sure" Toni responded, relieved that she was not brining bad news to a wife or girlfriend.

"Can we come in we need to ask you a few questions about Mr. Grey."

She moved in front of them behind her son and beckoned them to enter. "Please go in the sitting room there I'll just unpack a bit, I have frozen food that should go in the fridge ok."

They nodded and went into the room she had indicated. It was simply furnished with the usual stuff, sofas, sideboard, TV and a bookcase full of bits and pieces. They didn't sit down just waited for her to return. She was only a few minutes and asked them to be seated.

"Mrs ...?"

"Robinson, Joan Robinson, how can I help"

Toni began

'Thank you Mrs. Robinson we understand Gerry Grey lived here with you, what is your relationship and what else can you tell me about him?'

"He was our lodger he had the spare room, we needed a bit extra for the mortgage you know how it is. He was with us for almost a year now. He was quiet no trouble that is until three weeks ago when he left without a word.

He sometimes didn't come home for a night or two so didn't think anything of it at first but then I found some of my jewelry missing and my husbands gold watch, it was his Dad's. My God he was mad about that. Gerry left without paying his rent too.

We didn't report it we thought he would be miles away. What else has he done to bring you here?"

"I have to inform you that Mr. Grey has been found dead and we trying to trace his recent movements"

"Wow....that's a shock, I know he diddled us a bit but I wouldn't wish that on anyone he was nice mostly, what happened how did he die?"

"We don't know yet but it was not from natural causes. May we see his room please."

'The other men took his stuff so there's nothing to see, I've cleaned it ready to let again but you're welcome to look."

Alarm bells were ringing for Toni

"What do you mean other men?"

"The guys from his work, they came looking for him said he hadn't been to work. I told them what he'd done. They said he owed them too, asked if they could see his room. They took his clothes, TV and a few other things in his suitcase. I didn't mind I wanted the room cleared anyway."

"That's all right we'll still have a look, Peter will you...."

"It's the one straight in from of you at the top of the stairs" said Mrs. Robinson indicating to DC Andrews with a wave of her hand.

Peter returned a few minutes later looked at Toni and shook his head. "We'll need to talk to your husband at sometime when will he be home?"

"Not for a couple of hours yet what shall I tell him?"

"Please ask him to phone the police station tomorrow, thank you Mrs. Robinson I'm sorry for your loss, well arrange to come by again at your convenience"

" Ok I'll tell him..er do you think we might get back our stuff.. it's just the watch...you see my husband treasured it so?"

"If we come across it we will certainly return it but I don't hold out much hope, sorry"

Toni and Peter left and sat in their car a few minutes to digest the information obtained here.

"We need to go to his place of work but before we do we must see what sergeant Mann has found out and must have a definite cause of death. If it's a suicide we don't need to do much more but if it's a homicide we need to tread carefully. We don't want to spook any possible suspects. Lets go back to the station now."

When they arrived Fred Mann was sitting at his desk typing. Toni immediately questioned him

"Hello Sergeant what did you find out?"

"I'm just doing my report now" pointing at the computer screen. Toni looked at Fred with raised eyebrows indicating she need a verbal response

"Yes...well.... when I arrived there were just three guys working on site. It's a barn like workshop with an office inside and a front open show area. They had eleven cars out front with two in the garage. I took their registration numbers. A young lad Henry Starr, a trainee, who just cleaned the cars and did odd jobs, a sales man Kenneth Colins and the manager Philip Kaley. The owner Terry Owens who apparently doubles as the firm's mechanic wasn't there; I have his phone number and address but thought I'd come back here before going any further. They knew that Gerry Grey was missing, the manager was pretty angry though as he had found out that Gerry had been dealing on the side and had cost them a lot of money. He'd done a runner just about the time that he'd been sussed. They went round to his digs but his landlady had told them he had already left a couple of days before, apparently owing rent. That's about it, I didn't tell them he was dead just that we were looking for him with a connection to something else. I didn't notice there were any uncomfortable signs from any of them. I think they are just ordinary working blokes"

"That's good Fred, did they mention that they took all his stuff away from his digs?"

"No that's something they didn't give up. We need cause of death don't you think ma'am before we go on that is?"

"Yes I'm of the same mind. Andrews start writing up the report on our visit to his house. See what you can find out about the garage employees and check on those car numbers. I'll go and give the chief an update of where we are now and see if he has the Pathologist's results"

Fred went back to finishing his report, he hated uncompleted paperwork, it was the lifeblood of a case and he always tried to be ahead whilst it was fresh in his mind. He was glad that the incoming DI had the same work ethic; it boded well for this new team.

Peter went to his desk to fire up his computer and set himself ready for the tasks in hand. It was often the little things that broke a case and if this did turn out to be a murder he would make sure he left nothing to chance.

"Come in" was the response to Toni's knock on the DCI's door. "Ah..It's you, have a seat Webb where are we with this?" Toni then gave the Chief a summary of what had transpired with her and Fred's visits. "Do you have any information from the Pathologist Sir"?

"Nothing yet I'll give her another call now"

He picked up the phone and pressed the speakerphone facility and hit the speed dial number for Debbie Taylor's mobile. She answered almost at once.

"Yes...Chief Inspector I was about to call you. I do have some results for you. I'll send you the full report over the net. The important fact is that Mr. Gerry Grey was killed by a lethal injection of a cocktail of two anesthetic type drugs. The injection site was in the right hand side of his neck. The quantity of drug would have meant his death was almost instantaneous. One thing's for sure it could not have been self administered, the blood on the discarded paper handkerchief found at the scene indicated that the neck had been cleaned by a third party, so you may have a homicide on your hands. There are some other small oddities in the report but significantly we found some traces of money under the nails of his left hand. Torn pieces from fifty-pound notes. It appears that the money was pulled from his clenched fist at the time of his death or soon after. It would appear that Mr. Grey had been sexually active in the previous twelve hours, I have traces of some female DNA material from under his foreskin, however no match on our database. Perhaps some young lady would be missing him and report it"

'Thanks for that Doctor. What were the drugs used?

'The combination of Midaziolam and Diazepam was the main causes of the death. There were signs of other recreational drugs but they had no bearing on his death. It's all in the report it should be with you any moment. By the way the body has not been officially identified yet, we only have his name from fingerprint and stuff in his wallet. In addition to the wallet and other items found on him at the time of discovery we came across a train ticket stub deep in his trouser pocket, it was issued for the day he died and was a single from London Bridge. I'll send all his belongings over to you today. By the way his body has not been formally identified, we are relying on his drivers license and finger prints, pretty conclusive I know but a formal ID would leave no doubt "

"Thanks for all that you have been very thorough as usual. Ok yes you are right about the ID don't want the C.P.S, on our backs for being slack eh? Things are moving fast for us here but I will find someone who knew him to come to you with one of our officers for the ID."

He thanked her once again and hung up.

"Well well two of the drugs that she just mentioned were also found in the young girl in hospital." Toni stood up "This is no coincidence, first the finger print on the key and now identical drug cocktails found in both victims. We have something much bigger than we thought. How do you want to handle this sir?'

"We need to bring in the other team on this, call a meeting a.s.a.p. for everyone available. I'll put together a plan of action. Let me know when everyone can be here."

Toni was not daunted by being thrown in at the deep end of what seemed to be developing into a major case. She needed to make her mark here and this case was going to be her opportunity.

Toni was born in Nigeria; her parents were from the mid-west who had been at starvation point during the Biafra war. She and her brother survived as young children this terrible civil war of the 1960s. They were from the Ibo people and the near genocide of her Nation had made them wary of the tribal rivalries that had caused the bloody war and were fearful of it coming to a head again. At the first opportunity the Abakoba family Joseph, Maru, Dan and the baby Toni had emmigrated to England living in London initially. Her father was poorly educated but her mother had been to college in Ibadan where she qualified in biology. Her qualification was not acceptable as it was but she was able to re-train in England and eventually became a pharmacist whilst her father was a labourer on building sites. He supported the family whilst her mother went back to school for two years. He was strong and intelligent and soon learnt the trades from his fellow workers to the point where he became an excellent plasterer.

Young Dan and later Toni Abakoba were given the finest education they could afford as they, by their hard work, had proven that this was the way to progress in their new land.

The family moved to Southampton where her father set up his own business and her mother went to work for Boots the Chemists. Her brother went to university and eventually became a chemist but unlike like his mother he worked in research for a drug company.

Toni was a clever girl with good grades that enabled her to pass three A levels. She achieved a place at Winchester Technical College to study structural engineering. It was whilst at college that she met Laurence Webb. Larry was one year ahead of Toni, studying computer science. He graduated ahead of her and went to work for Vospers the shipbuilding company. Toni left college a year later and moved in with Larry at his flat in Gosport. They married the following year, much to the relief of her parents who were a little old fashioned in their ways. Toni fell pregnant soon after but miscarried at month four. They tried again with no luck so put on hold the plans for a family.

Toni seemed quite philosophical about not being able to have children so decided to do "something useful" as she put it. She became a part time community police officer near her home. Since then a full time WPC with training at Hendon. Later sergeant. She transferred to Criminal Investigation at Southampton some years later and was promoted to DI two years before this current transfer to Basingstoke. Her record of successfully solved cases and especially murder made her a prime candidate for promotion, which she was not expecting to come too soon, as there was some jealouses at work not in her favour.

The transfer away from Southampton was at her request as her marriage had suffered partly due to the long hours she worked as a police officer but more because of the strain of being childless. She pretended that it didn't matter but deep down she was hurting. Larry was attentive but had lately given up trying to please her as nothing seemed to work. She loved him dearly but neglected his needs and rejected his kindness. The split was inevitable; they agreed a trial separation would be best, so here she was hiding away in Basingstoke nick. Work was to be her salvation she hoped. She would go back and be a better wife later when her ambitions had been fulfilled or she gave up trying.

She was renting a small house in Chineham in a quiet village type overspill development of Basingstoke. It was only ten minutes from the station but beacause the builders had kept the woodland around the development it felt as if you were in a country setting. She loved her choice, it was so different to her larger terraced house in a crowded area of Southampton. From the day she moved in her neighbours were offering her tea and cakes plus any help she might need to establish herself. She was quickly informed where the doctors surgery was located, the best place for take away curry and where the path through the woods lay that was a short cut to Tescos. She had lived in Southampton for years but didn't even hardly speak to those that lived next door, here she had met and was welcomed by at least five of her close neighbours in just a few days. Perhaps this was the place that would heal her hurt.

Chapter 25

Toby was a happy man and a soon to be very rich one. The Fairchiled woman was well out of the way and that good for nothing Gerry character had been dispatched.

He wasn't jealous of Gerry and Sandra's relationship, he knew it was just a means to an end. If Sandra had a bit of fun out of it too good luck to her. His feeling towards Sandra were different. He cared for her in his own way, she was clever resourceful fun to be with many other laudable traits, but he had no sexual desire towards her or any female for that matter. Something else attracted her to him and him to her neither of them knew what but it was strong and powerful like two electro magnets. Whatever the reason Sandra was back to do his bidding once again. She had changed somehow; he couldn't put his finger on it. Always confident and subservient as before but with a hint of bravado, not previously seen which was disquieting for Toby.

Sandra had given Toby a detailed account of the abduction and staged accident. She also told him how Gerry had been put to rest. He thought he had the full picture but she had omitted her feelings of sadistic pleasure enjoyed in the cellar, and the cock-ups made by Gerry at the staged accident. She thought they were safe enough and he would be none too pleased if he thought something was awry.

He didn't push for more information just glad that her reports had lain to rest their problems, for now at least.

The sale of WW would be concluded tomorrow morning, the money could be transferred to his offshore accounts the same day. He could stay in England for a while at least or go if he wanted. He would contact his man to see how things stood on that front.

Chapter 26

DCI Craig Bean stood tall in front of his officers his head full of rambling thoughts. Now was the time for consolidation and focus. He was waiting for everyone to arrive and settle, thinking how long it was since he'd had a case as complex as this one was turning out to be. Basingstoke was a relatively quiet patch. A mixture of villains and low level criminals, domestic disputes, driving offences and not much more. The last murder was three years before; another escalated domestic fight, which got out of hand, soon solved. It seemed everyone who needed to be was here now.

"Right listen up...we have a complex case here with all of you needing to work together if we are to get anywhere soon. DI Dale and his team have just apprehended Welbrooke who has confessed to the burglaries in his current case so his team will be free very soon. Colin do your best to wind up the paperwork there and liaise with the C.P.S. DI Webb could really do with your help a.s.a.p."

"Yes boss, DS Musgrove can handle what's left there, two days tops. Mel and I will be free as from now. It won't go to court for ages but I may have to give the C.P.S. lawyers a bit of my time now and then. Anything we can do to help here just say the word."

"That's good Colin, work with DI Webb on task allocation she'll take the lead on this as her team are already well into the case"

"Sir..." Colin accepted the situation a bit disgruntled that the newby was given lead on what would probably be the biggest case he had seen in years. He would bide his time, let her make the mistakes and look for his opportunity to step in.

"Everyone needs to be up to speed with what has happened recently so I called you all here just to do that."

The white board behind Craig Bean was part covered in photos and bits of data in black marker. By the time this case was finished it would be covered completely.

"First, for those of you who don't know him this is Detective Chief Inspector Henry Jakes an expert in accident investigation. He is the head of Hampshire AI unit based in Alton....Henry"

Henry stood and nodded to the room.

"Well...we still have one or two item outstanding but this is what we have so far. It seems likely the truck and car came from the same source, both ringed with false plates from valid identical type vehicles. All traces, well nearly all, of original ID have been removed, however the clincher linking them together were the palm prints found on the chassis of both vehicles being from the same person. Although gloves were worn during the theft, de-numbering and use of the vehicle one mechanic was not so careful as he left his handprint on the chassis as he slid himself out from under. The truck left nothing else to find except that there was nothing wrong with it. The flat battery was due to the lights and hazards being left on for several hours, it clearly had not broken down as was first thought. The VW Golf was different as it had electronics that was original. We have a difficult problem tracing the ID through this and it is still ongoing. The steering and door locks were changed however with a new key, this led to the car self locking mechanism operating when parked after having been moved. The new key did not match the existing electronics, a mistake that, in my opinion, led to the scenario I am about to describe. The whole accident was staged. I believe the truck was left deliberately in that spot. The car was driven slowly into the back of the truck by the unknown driver. More of him in a minute. He exited the car shut his door and left with his passenger unconscious. Why he didn't move her to the drivers side I don't know but suspect the auto self-locking scotched his plans to do so. He could not have got into the car once it had locked because he foolishly had left the key in the ignition. There must have been another vehicle to take him away, the site is quite isolated. We are almost certain the driver was Gerry Grey as his print was found on the key fob. That's where we are for now, we are still working on the true IDs but don't expect that will help much as they are probably stolen from legitimate owners."

"Thanks Henry..any question anyone?"

"Any joy with the hand print?" piped up Colin Dale

"Not yet, nothing on our database, could of course be a genuine mechanic who happened to work on both vehicles prior to their being stolen but I don't believe in miracles or coincidences"

Colin continued "Any witness information at the scene"

Henry responded again

"Constable Andrews was first at the scene they were interviewed on site by him but were shook up and did not have much to offer at the time. He did follow up later and found out that they had seen a motorbike travelling towards them, on reflection they thought it strange that he did not stop at the scene of the accident, as he must have passed it a few moments before. It's all in his report. It may have been Gerry Grey making his escape. We are searching CCTV as we speak, we may find something."

Craig looked hard at Colin Dale understanding what he was trying to do.

"Lets move on... DI Andrews where are we with the girl in hospital?"

" Sir....she is conscious now but has no recollection of anything, doesn't even know her name. She says Harriet then Mary but no surname she did say her office was on Marlborough Road London nothing more. Doctor Mike Smith hopes to stimulate her memory with hypnotherapy soon. She has had a massive cocktail of drugs some still in her system. Some they know about, some they don't. I've arranged for a blood sample taken when she was first admitted to be sent to the pathologist who also found drugs in Gerry Grey, which were a match in some ways to hers. The pathologist will call me when she has had time to study the sample, I don't know when."

"Did you get a picture lad?"

"Yes Sir, I took one at the hospital. I photo-shopped it to get rid of the medical paraphernalia, it looks ok now"

"Right... circulate that to the local papers with 'a do you know this girl' caption do what's necessary, you never know the Nationals may pick it up. We may be lucky someone somewhere must be missing her this girl did not live in isolation" Craig paused a minute to let everyone, including himself, digest the information.

"Ok... Fred what have you got"

Fred took out his notebook, he hated to rely on memory alone you could so easily miss something important.

" Gerry Grey was a small time intermittent crook minor infringements mostly shoplifting the worst. No time served. Most recently he has lived and worked in Basingstoke for about a year. Kept his nose clean until three weeks ago when he up and left his digs taking valuables from the landlord and without paying his rent. He left his job too. He was a car salesman with Westwood Motors; they had discovered since his departure he had been working a fiddle on the sales. When they found out they went round his house to find him gone. They took some of his stuff away as compensation for their loss. The landlady didn't object she just wanted the room clear so she could relet. They could be suspects but I doubt it. I interviewed them at length and although he owed both of them they are really ordinary folks who may have given him a good hiding if they had caught up with him, premeditated murder is unlikely.

I found the two boys who reported the body to the park keeper. They were only nine years old and a tad nervous of me, anyway I did get one piece of information from them, they thought they saw him talking to a woman, no proper description though just dressed in black with a black bag, they weren't even sure of that. One did touch him however, he thought he was asleep; he got a shock when Gerry keeled over eyes open, scared the poor little buggers out of their skins, they then ran to the park keeper. I've collected the CCTV footage from the area none overlooking the park though. No results yet. That's about it."

"Thank you sergeant, now Constable Busion any news from you yet?"

"I'm still going through the CCTV footage sir, there's hours of it but nothing stands out so far, not even scratched it yet....."

Craig interrupted him.

" Colin get Detective Constable Frazer to help there... sorry Compton please go on"

"Yes sir, been checking on Gerry Greys cards and phone. The phone is a new pay as you go and hardly used just a couple of local calls. His office and home. The cards are more revealing, he has used them in London over the last three weeks the odd taxi and ATMs in Shorditch and a garage in Hammersmith the day before the accident. I have the CCTV from the garage, I can't see his face as he kept it covered by a hood and faced away whenever near the cameras especially at the till. Good news though the car he used was a blue VW Golf reg number

DA12NNM. I have contacted the taxi firms to find out pick-up and drop-off addresses. Some have records some don't, one address comes up more than once it is a warehouse in Shoreditch. The detailed search of his clothes by the pathologist turned up some hairs not belonging to him and a train ticket wedged in the bottom of a trouser pocket. It was a London to Portsmouth one way issued on the morning he died"

"Good job there Compton a confirmation that Gerry Grey was probably the missing driver."

Toni decided that now was the time to step in and take charge at least a little. It was obvious that DI Colin Dale was a little put out at being second fiddle to new DI, a woman too and a black one at that. She didn't know if he was prejudiced or not but felt the unhappy vibe.

She needed him on her side not only for the case but also for her future in this station. Ignoring the fact that the DCI was standing behind her she took her first assertive step.

"With this obvious London and Shoreditch connection it might be a good idea to have her picture circulated in the city. Colin I have no experience of London or how we could go about that what do you think" This was not really true as she had plenty of friends in the Met however she wanted him to feel involved to the level of his rank her having just been handed the role of S.I.O.

The use of his first name was a familiarity Colin Dale was not expecting, the question posed also relinquished some of her superiority to him. Perhaps this partnership could take a better turn.

"I good idea...err....Toni" he hesitated to continue the familiarity but was into it now. "I have contacts with the Standard an evening paper that's available at all London stations daily, I'll get her picture in for tomorrow"

"Great I knew you had the nonce to make this case progress quickly, OK everyone lets digest and discuss with your colleagues what we have learnt today. Have a coffee or tea or whatever, we will reconvene this meeting in twenty minutes"

Almost everyone made a beeline for the canteen the rest moved to their desks or places of work. Toni turned to the white board maker in hand.

She turned to Craig and smiled. " I hope that is all right with you sir another few hours and we should have a handle on this...eh?"

Craig smiled back and nodded, then walked back into his office, he was glad he had taken on this woman she had balls.

"Right everyone come to order please...." The background hubbub ceased after a couple of seconds.

"This is where I think we are" pointing to the now updated white board. "If there is anything you think I've missed please feel free to interject before I move on to the next topic.

First the staged accident, we now know from the AIU that the car and van are stolen stripped of their true identity and have been ringed with false but real plates. The insurance documents and MOTs of the genuine vehicles gave them apparent legitimacy.

This was not done by amateurs a largish bent workshop is involved here, probably outside Hampshire, London and the suburbs is a good bet. Sergeant Musgrove please follow up with the usual suspects through your and DI Dale's contacts in the MET use Gerry Greys photo to see if he has been a ‘customer’. A long shot I know but try and get a match for the handprint.”

Sergeant Jonny Musgrove got the nod of approval from his DI and responded.

“ Yes Ma’am, I will start in Hammersmith seeing as how Gerry was spotted there getting petrol”

“Good yes spread the net wider if you have no joy there” She turned and added the Hammersmith sighting to the board as a link to the car jackers.

“Gerry Grey is now confirmed as the driver by both his print on the key fob and the garage CCTV two days before the accident. He was in Basingstoke on the day of the accident and was found dead the following day in the park. Where was he during the two days before? We know he also was in Shoreditch around this time and was involved with a woman or girl other than Miss Noname from the hair and DNA found on his body. He died of drug injections very similar to those found in our hospital victim. We need to find the unknown woman seen with him in the park and who may be his lover and even his killer.

Constable Busion please continue with your work on the CCTV data along with DC Frazer. Widen the search to earlier times a week or so if still available. Officers please forward any footage found during you investigations at other locations."

She turned towards Colin and beckoned him forward.

" I am new to this nick so will rely heavily on Detective Inspector Dale here to make sure I do not miss a trick so please pass all information to him as well as me. Colin please will you follow up on the Shoreditch address and try to get some CCTV of the area. Interview the taxi guys you know what to do. I would inform the local DCI or Super that you will be on their patch, I'm sure you know the best guy for that. By the way did you get her picture in the papers yet"

"Yes to that, both the local and the London Standard this evening, phone number is this station for any calls, I'll tell the switch board to route pertinent calls to Melanie and Compton here OK?"

"That's great thanks, see if you can find out this Malborough Road office, it may be just the ramblings of a crazy girl; knock on doors show her picture we may get lucky"

She stood back and looked at the white-board again making sure she was covering every lead.

"Fred and Peter you can re-check all the witnesses for the sighting of the woman and Gerry Grey. Go back to where he worked they probably know more than they are saying. There is a possibility they travelled by train, check at the station and points between there and the park. Get any CCTV footage for the times in question and a bit before if you can. Peter you can go through the autopsy report in detail, find out about the drugs where they can be bought, any skills or special equipment needed to administer them."

She looked round to see if anyone had anything to add.

"Ok. That's it I think. I'm going to the hospital, Harriet Jane Noname is the key to this and needs to give us some answers. Thanks everyone; don't forget keep in touch."

Craig Bean stayed in his office with the door slightly ajar so he could hear what was going on. He timed leaving to coincide with Toni's departure.

"Good job DI Webb just what was needed a bit of push and a touch of diplomacy. Don't take on too much though, remember I'm here too, keep me up to date eh"

"Of course sir I think we have a good chance of progress today"

"Let us hope so Toni…let us hope so…"

Chapter 27

Toby was now about to make his decision, would he stay or go? Before then he needed a clearer picture of what was going on out there.

Sandra was being too positive about the whole affair, and now there was plenty of money and no company ties left to hold them here she wanted to book tickets to exotic places without regard for the consequences. He was more cautious however and did not trust her reports about how the ties to them were gone forever. He still had property here and would like to have the use of it whenever he wanted, which would not be possible if he left. He did not need to be looking over his shoulder every five minutes. Peace of mind was his goal, wherever he might land up.

He would call his tame PI to search Miss Fairbanks's flat for anything that Sandra and Gerry had missed. He had her computer and memory cards, plus some files all of which he had destroyed. There could easily be more and maybe some files at her office that could be a problem. "Let's see what

Joseph finds at her flat first before we go there" he said to himself.

He was very unsure of what had transpired in Basingstoke. He hated to be in the dark so intended to renew an old 'friendship' from early London days who now lived in Hampshire. He would at least have a handle on where any investigation might be going and could maybe deflect it if it started to get a little too close. He would make that phone call this evening; first thing though to give Private Investigator Joseph his instructions.

The documents that may lead to his deception being revealed were gradually being destroyed, the remaining ones that he knew of resided in the Land Registry Office. He decided to go there and deal with that himself.

Chapter 28

Fred was helping Fiona into bed when the phone rang.

"Damn, I must get an extension up here" he thought. He knew by the time he got downstairs it would have stopped ringing so he didn't bother to try.

"It's probably work love, they'll call back" he said replying to his wife's questioning look.

"Will you have to go out? I'll be all right for a bit on my own you know you don't have to call anyone in" Fiona knew how difficult it was for Fred to leave her unattended.

"I don't think so Fi they are just trying to keep me up to date I expect. There's nothing that can't wait until tomorrow. Anything I can get you before I go down?"

No thanks Fred I'm ok now ta"

He pecked her on the cheek and patted her shoulder. "Sleep tight eh"

He closed the door halfway before heading downstairs.

The nightly ritual of helping Fiona up the stairs and into bed was becoming more and more difficult as she slowly lost control of her body. Not a dead weight yet but very weak and unsteady. He should consider having a stair lift or maybe even moving to a bungalow something would have to be done soon.

Fred went into the kitchen, grabbed a can of speckled hen from the fridge and settled in his old chair with the paper. Here it was nearly ten o'clock and this was the first time he'd had a minute to himself since sunrise. If only he was stronger or younger or both he would cope. The pending retirement was often uppermost in his mind but it would have to wait for now. Fred was resigned to his lot.

The phone rang again. "I knew it, just as I sat down" he grumbled to himself.

"What time do you call this?" he spoke into the phone jokingly thinking it was young Andrews keeping him in the loop.

Fred choked on his words and an ice cold shiver ran down his spine when he heard the voice at the end of the line.

"Hello Manny long time no see"

His mind shot back thirty years to when he was a beat copper in London. Fred was truly shocked.

"What the hell do you want?" he barked.

"That's no way to speak to an old friend. Just a courtesy call to see how you are"

"I'm fine. Now what do you really want?"

"Nothing much Manny old chum just wondered if you have anything exciting going on down your way that's all. I'll call you some time tomorrow to arrange a little get together for old times sake. Keep your mobile on you"

The phone went dead. Fred stood there with the phone handset held to his ear menacing in its silence.

Fred and Toby came to be acquaintances as young men when drinking in the same pub in Camberwell. This shifted over time to becoming mates if not real friends. Drinking, playing snooker, darts and the odd card school were their common past-times.

Fred foolishly trusted Toby even though he knew he sailed close to the wind when it came to his earning a living. He was more than generous, always had plenty of cash and did not seem to go to work much.

As a young policeman Fred studied his seniors and was encouraged by them in their dubious ways of operating. Many officers mixed socially with the criminal element with a view to nurturing informants. Fred thought this was normal and approved; he naively followed their lead.

Toby had his ear to the ground of the criminal fraternity and often helped Fred with information which he passed on to his DI leading to some significant arrests, which more than pleased his senior officers.

When Toby was being looked at by the fraud squad for some housing scam he managed to convince Fred that he was being set up. Fred used his influence to deflect the attention away from Toby and towards the people that Toby had named.

Fred made the mistake of accepting a 'gift' of thanks for helping him. Five hundred pounds was a small fortune to Fred and although he knew it was not right, temptation was too strong. He told himself it was just between friends so no harm done. How wrong he was.

He learnt later that Toby was in fact the one responsible and those prosecuted had been set up by him to take the fall. Too late for Fred to do anything about that he had been turned.

From then on Toby used Fred as a source of inside information on several occasions, each time providing Fred with a grateful 'gift'.

On moving to Basingstoke Fred thought he had put that all behind him and set his sights on becoming a good copper. Toby had other ideas and continued to demand his help through Fred's London contacts. This continued for some years but had eventually ceased as Fred's contacts in the MET dried up with the fullness of time. Fred had been left alone for several years but now the 'devil' had come home.

He lay awake all night wondering what Toby wanted. He knew it must be something to do with the Gerry Grey murder or the girl or both. He rationalised that if he only wanted information it wouldn't be too bad, this time however he would ensure that he was well paid, maybe enough for him to quit at last.

The call came the next morning Fred said nothing just listened. "Take the nineteen fifty Basingstoke to London train, get off at Esher and wait on the platform. My man will meet you. Bring everything you have on the investigation into the two cases, you know which ones without me telling you. He will give you a mobile phone take it but never use it. I will call you on it once then destroy it. You will be well paid. If you do this right I will never contact you again." The phone went dead. Fred never had the chance to say anything nor indeed did he want to. What to do? He had little choice. " I'm going out for a couple of hours dear" he called up the stairs, you'll be all right won't you.

"Where are you going love, when will you be back?"

"Just a bit of business I won't be too late I'll bring us in some fish and chips for supper"

"That'll be nice I'd like that, I'll be fine for a while"

"Bye then" He closed the door taking the file he had composed earlier. It contained the names dates and evidence that had been collected over the last few days. Why Toby had an interest in these cases he did not know or even care.

Esher station was quite busy; he had left the train some ten minutes before and sat waiting on a seat adjacent to where his carriage had stopped. Fred suspected the 'man' whoever he was, would arrive on the next down train on another platform. It seemed forever the waiting, he almost dozed off.

His reverie was disturbed by a man who sat next to him quietly but too close to be anyone but his expected contact.

Joseph spoke. "Put your stuff in this bag. Wait ten minutes after I've gone, take the newspaper and phone I will leave on this seat. You will be contacted."

Fred put the file in the plastic bag. With that Joseph was gone.

Fred waited a while then picked up his package, crossed to the other platform to take the train home. His betrayal was complete. He was a mess.

A brave face was his when he arrived home. With the fish supper under his arm" I'm back dear"

No reply "she's asleep, I'll go up" he thought. He put the take-away in a low oven to keep warm and climbed the stairs.

Fred looked at his sleeping wife wondering where all the time had gone and for what. He loved her dearly but would she love him knowing what he had become? He gave a light shake to her shoulder. She awoke with a smile for him.

"Hello love you weren't long it only seems like you'd just gone out."

"Yes dear all done now I'll bring your supper up on a tray if you like it's a bit late to come down again" He dreaded the down and up, up and down day after day, and was glad when she agreed.

"That will be nice dear can I have a cuppa with that?"

"Sure Fi, back in a minute."

He prepared the meal and decided to eat his supper sitting beside her on the bed. The two of them sat in silence munching away. He enjoyed this simple being together, why couldn't it always be like this.

After they'd finished he tucked her in, said goodnight and went down stairs, cleared the things away and moved to sit in his usual chair suddenly remembering the envelope wrapped in the newspaper along with the phone which he'd dumped on the hall table, unlooked at until now.

The phone was a basic pay as you go, he saw that it was charged and active. He was tempted to destroy it then and there and cut all ties with Toby but he knew that could not happen so he put it in his overcoat pocket. He discarded the newspaper and looked at the sealed, fat, brown padded envelope. Inside he wasn't surprised to find three bunches of twenty, fifty-pound notes. Three grand, quite a lot considering for one file of information but not much for a ruined life. He had forgotten that he was going to demand a big payoff, the situation and Toby's threat to his existence overpowered him as it always had. He looked at the cash, he would have that stair lift fitted now, at least some good would come of it.

He would put in his resignation tomorrow, Fiona and he would manage somehow. He reached for the brandy bottle, he would need a little help if he were to sleep tonight.

The call came the next morning in the form of a text.

'Goodbye Manny old chum you won't see me again just a name for you to do with as you wish Sandra Cooper.'

That was all. Fred deleted the text and then used the phone and made the call. He removed the sim card cut it into pieces and threw it in the bin. He would dump the phone in the canal on his way in to work.

Let that be an end to it I've had enough.

Chapter 29

DI Webb was seated in a chair in the lounge set aside for visitors. It was often used by patients with their families partly for privacy but also for a little more comfort than was available on the ward. Mike was sitting opposite explaining the procedure that they were going to use to push Harriet's mind to open up from its hiding place.

"Detective please remember what ever happens you must not speak. You won't be able to ask questions at this stage, we have to control the trauma that will be revealed or she could slip back even deeper into herself. We hope that small steps in this type of treatment will save this young girl from permanent damage."

Next to Toni sat the young nurse who had been tending Harriet from the beginning. Mike returned some minutes later with Harriet, he sat her in an armchair with her back to the detective and nurse. He then proceeded to explain the mysterious circumstances of her 'accident' and subsequent arrival in hospital. He told her of the drugs that had caused her to be in a coma and had probably caused her memory loss.

" I can't explain any of that" she said " the only thing that stands out are the bad dreams I keep having they seem so real, I don't even want to think about it"

" Look we are not getting anywhere at the moment by waiting for you to get better, we need to be more positive if you are to recover your memory. A doctor on the staff here has some experience in these matters. I will ask him to come by if that is ok with you, I am sure he can help"

" Anything you like doctor, I can't stay like this it's not natural"

Mike left her and went to the nurses station to make the pre-arranged call to Doctor Bridge who was standing by.

Harriet sat quietly unaware of the presence of the other two in the room. Mike returned some short time later.

" Harriet this is Doctor Bridge he is the one going to help you?"

" Hello Harriet, My name is Mark Bridge I'm going to ask you a few questions before we start. Do you mind if I touch your hands"

"No I don't think so"

"Good, are you happy for me to help you remember?"

"Yes of course anything..."

He took her hands which were in her lap and gently placed them on the arms of the chair "Fine, now I want you to relax in your body, settle into the seat, rest your arms, it is very very comfortable and safe. Your whole being is sinking into it's softness you are so tired now....your eyelids are heavy.... let your eyes close... you are now falling into a deep deep sleep..One... two... three...four....five" Mark Bridge waited a full minute before speaking again.

"Can you hear me Harriet?"

"Yes I can hear you"

"Good, now I want you to go back to your last morning at home, where are you?"

" I'm in the kitchen I've just got up I'm having a juice..must leave for work soon"

"Are you late for work?"

"No I'm never late"

“Good....now let us move on a while where are you, what are you doing?”

“I’m at my desk I am working on my files”

“That’s fine now let’s move on again. It’s been a long day at work let’s go. Where are you now?”

“I’m walking home”

“Are you late...what is your name....where do you live?”

“I’m never late. I’m Harriet Fairbanks, number seven Squires Muse...I’m nearly home but what is this, something’s wrong in the lift...”

“What is wrong Harriet?”

“The man is sick he has collapsed I must help”

“Good where are you now?”

“ I don’t know....the black room, no..no I don’t want to be here” She suddenly let out a terrifying scream, making everyone in the room jump, then she started sobbing uncontrollably.

“Bridge took her hand and started stroking her arm, counting down. “Five....four..three....two..one”

Harriet awoke tears streaming down her cheeks, for the moment unaware of what had just happened.

“There you are “ said Doctor Bridge giving her a tissue for her eyes “You did very well”

"I d...did?" she stuttered "What happened?"

" Your name please?"

"Harriet Mary Fairbanks... yes...that's me...I remember...thank you...thank you..."

"Do you know where you live?"

"Of course.. it's...its.."

Bridge prompted her not wanting to lose the momentum " Number seven.."

"Seven Squires Muse.. yes that's it"

Suddenly a dark looking frown came across her face.

"Oh my God..that place...that evil woman with the needles...keep her away from me...I cannot go back there...I can't please... "

It took a while to calm Harriet down as memories of her ordeal came back. Mike moved her back to her bed and administered a mild sedative. She was afraid to sleep but eventually drifted off thankfully into a dreamless sleep.

Mike went back to the side room where Toni was making notes on what she had just witnessed.

"Thank you detective for not reacting to that. Dr. Bridge is one of the best so we must follow his lead,

I'm sure the information gleaned here will help you move forward"

"That's for sure" replied Toni "If these are real memories this girl has been severely abused and traumatised by this woman, it would be nice to have a description maybe next time. Thanks for letting me stay and please keep me informed of anything new that you learn, you have my mobile don't you?"

"Yes I do, don't worry I know our aims are different here but information to help you catch this vile person will be yours as soon as I have it. It may be some time before I can allow you to interview her though, you will be the first I contact as soon as it is safe for her"

"Thanks Doctor..... look after her" with that Toni left she had lots to do now.

Chapter 30

Toni called the meeting to order.

"Right everyone listen up. We will soon be in a position to move in on our suspects. First we had some thirty responses to the news paper picture of the girl. Four of these turned out to be genuine. We now know her name Harriet Jane Fairbanks where she lives and her office.

She is a freelance forensic accountant who has been investigating some various dubious dealings. She has obviously stirred up same nasty characters that wanted her out of the way. She has also recovered a little. Her abduction lead to chemical torture used to try and destroy her memory or extract information maybe both we don't know. The torture was inflicted by a woman.

The link between Gerry Grey and Harriet is now established without doubt. He was to stage an accident with her as the victim, it didn't go too well so we did not buy into it as they thought we would.

Gerry obviously upset his masters and was executed for his efforts, we suspect by a woman who was seen at the time of his murder. We have CCTV of one such female who was seen near the station a short time after the killing. Earlier footage some days before also places the same woman on Basingstoke station the same time as Gerry Grey. Her description and an e-fit picture has been circulated this was done partly from a child witness and from the poor quality CCTV images. Not perfect but we did get one anonymous response. The name Sandra Cooper.

Harriet's computer, phone, keys and some files were removed from her person but a specific memory stick was found hidden by our forensics team when searching her flat.

The 'fact' that we are looking for a piece of missing digital evidence has been inserted as part of our press release along with the efit. We have left a duplicate hidden in the flat in the hope that someone will take the bait.

We will mount surveillance for a couple of days. All this information has come about by good team work from you all." Toni took a quick drink from her coldish coffee before continuing.

"DI Dale and DS Musgrove will start the surveillance, DC Frazer will go to Harriet's offices and find out what she has been working on that may have upset someone recently. Sergeant Mann will follow up tracing the woman and the drugs angle. DC Andrews and I will go to the Hospital and try to interview Harriet Fairbanks. We have had no good sightings from Shoreditch although Constable Busion is still to receive some of the CCTV. So keep on that Compton and look into that name Sandra Cooper if you will. Anything you get send through to the Chief. If there are no questions go to it" There were none. A quick shuffling of feet a few comments between colleagues and the squad room slowly emptied apart from Toni and Peter. " Just need to see the DCI before we go wait in the car for me please Peter"

"Did you get all that sir"

"Yes Toni, progress is good. The London connection is strong, I feel our area has been used as a dumping ground. It's a wonder the Met boys have not muscled in. I think DI Dale has had a lot to do with that sir, he has a lot of friends there and knows his way around there too."

"Aye you're right he does that, nice to see you two getting along, I thought it might be touch and go at first."

"No problem for me I bend with the wind, where I'm coming from I've had to do a lot of that, still it doesn't stop me from doing what's needed"

"Fair enough, keep me with it and yell if it gets out of hand. I'm here ok"

"Ok...sir"

"Where to Ma'am"

" The hospital please Peter"

Harriets memory had gradually been returning. The drugs had been purged from her system although the effects of the hullucogen would be with her for some time. Flashbacks and false memories were a long term side effect. It would take a strong mind to distinguish the real from the imagined. Treatment with Doctor Bridge was a great help in allowing her to relive and put to one side the horrors of her treatment by Sandra.

Toni had been visiting Harriet along with Peter to try and obtain a description of her abductors. She had provided a fairly good description of the woman but was unable to recall Gerry. Her very brief view of him on the floor of the lift was just that. They had questioned her about her recent studies which may have attracted this exceptional reaction. Who was in the most trouble from her investigations.

There were at least six different companies and individuals that were currently under scrutiny. The police had collected her files from her office but none stood out as being particularly significant.

They were being checked out by DC Busion one at a time. Although Toby was one of these the link from his personal oversaes transfers to the sale of WW Enterprises had not been made by Harriet. She had considered his offshore dealings so far were small fry and would come back to them later when she had dealt with more important cases.

Ironic that all this would not have been necessary if only Toby had waited. His sale of WW and the transfer of funds would have been completed long before Harriet had made the connection, indeed she may never have followed it up.

DC Busion had not put anything aside she had indeed found that the sale of WW Enterprises had netted David Charles Jones a huge personal payout which he had immediately transferred overseas to various accounts. Not exactly illegal but she wondered why would he sell such a fast growing and successful company, this needed a closer look. Not the small fry after all.

Chapter 31

Joseph climbed to the floor of flat seven via the stairs, he used the key Toby had given him. He didn't know exactly what he was looking for, anything paperwork or digital was all that Toby had said. He started with the bedroom; every drawer was carefully searched and replaced inside and under. He moved the bedside cabinet away from the wall. In and under the bed, under the rugs behind the pictures being careful to replace everything as he found it. Nothing so far. He continued to work his way through the flat examining every possible hiding place. He eventually found what he was looking for in the fridge. Wrapped in cling-film under a packet of bacon was a memory stick. "Crafty cow" he thought "Maybe there's more?" The living room and bathroom revealed no secrets. He sat in the armchair looking round going over his complete search to make sure he had missed nothing. " She seems to be a 'belt and braces person' there must be more probably in her office; that won't be easy" He did not have a key so would have to break in. It was occupied by several people throughout the day and sometimes quite late. He could only search at night he would see Toby first. He did one more check to make sure there was no evidence of his presence and left the way he came.

DI Colin Dale had been watching as Joseph entered her apartment block. Jonny Musgrove had the camera on full zoom. "Two good shots guv full face too" They waited till he left some forty minutes later. Another couple of timed shots were taken. "Do we follow him sir?"

"Yes give him a minute to get to his car. Joseph entered his Honda parked near the corner unaware of the officers nearby. They noted the registration number let him leave and followed at a safe distance. The London traffic made following with just one vehicle very difficult and not wishing to be spotted Colin decided to hang back.

Joseph parked outside the Young's Hotel as did DI Colin Dale a few minutes later.

Toby took the memory stick from Joseph and loaded it into his laptop. A multitude of files all with letter and number file names. He looked for those beginning with 'T', 'J' and 'WW' with no resulting data. He did a search with his name and the name of

W.W. Enterprises but came up with nothing. He opened file after file to be presented with spreadsheets and financial breakdowns but no names only coded letters and numbers. Without the key he had no way of identifying who the files related to. He looked to see if any of the data was recognisable. He found one file that showed him sums of money being transferred offshore; not his though. He knew it would take hours to decipher all the information, time he didn't have. He also knew it was probably a fake.

The information from Fred Mann told him they would be watching the girl's flat and deduced that Joseph had probably been followed to the hotel.

He spotted the unmarked police car from the window, the two occupants were not clearly visible but were obviously waiting for Joseph or maybe him to come out.

"Joseph forget about going to Fairbanks office I have enough here" waving the memory stick at him " I want you to destroy anything that ties us together" He then handed him a large envelope" Here's what we agreed plus a big bonus. I'll be going away for a while and suggest you do the same as I suspect the police may soon come asking questions"

Joseph took the envelope " Thanks for this and don't worry boss I know where my loyalties need to be, are you sure there is nothing else I can do for you?"

"I don't think so, except maybe Sandra will come looking I don't want her to find me understand."

"Sure, if she asks I haven't seen you for ages in any case I'll probably be away before she catches up with me. Oh and good luck Toby call me sometime."

A handshake and he was gone. Toby did not warn Joseph of the police presence outside. Toby thought he might need to slip away if they stopped him. He watched Joseph leave unaccompanied, so they were waiting for him.

Toby now knew that he had made the right decision in preparing to leave. Everything that could be sold had been. Almost all the funds had been transferred to private offshore accounts and would be moved again when he arrived overseas. He had drawn as much cash in Euros and American dollars as he could and would be gone tonight. He had already bought tickets to his final destination via three different stop-offs purchased under different names. First Europe then Africa on to Granada and finally South America. He had passports to cover these identities it would take someone a month of Sundays to follow that trail. A new identity a new name a new beginning.

Colin and Jonny sat in their car a few yards down the road and waited until Joseph came out some twenty minutes later.

"Let him go for now Jonny we have his details here" Colin had been searching the police vehicle database whilst Jonny was following the Honda. "Car's registered to a Joseph Mallard a private dick no less. I more interested in what he was doing here and who his client might be. Wait here Mel I'm going into the Hotel to see what's what."

DI Dale put on his official face and went up to the reception desk. He showed his warrant card to the young girl behind the desk.

"Can you please tell me to which room that man who just left had been"

She was a little taken back but his forthright manner elicited an automatic response repeating what Toby had told her. "That was room 203 a Mr. John Smith"

"Thank you, do you have any details"

She showed him the registration book with his unrecognisable signature. 'That's all I have" she said. "Did he pay with his credit card?"

"No, he paid cash in advance, he is due to check out anytime now"

He thanked her and told her not to mention his visit as the man was a suspect and did not want him warned. She nodded, Colin left.

He explained to Jonny what had transpired. "John Smith! I don't think so, we'll wait a bit to see who comes out" They didn't have to wait too long before a man emerged totally unaware he was being watched. Jonny took a full face shot as the man walked by. "Do you think that was him?" she asked

"I hope so" replied Colin "we won't have to wait any longer if it was. I'll go and check you follow him Mel and keep your phone open on" He crossed the road to where the receptionist was still at her counter. "Was that Mr. Smith who just left?" Following the Toby script Deena replied

"Yes...maybe..yes I think it was; he gave me a tip too are you sure he is a suspect he seemed very nice"

"The clever ones always do young lady, we'll see"

His bag was packed he walked down the stairs and went behind the reception desk into the office behind. "Hello Deena I need you to help me a little more"

"Oh Mr. Jones I did as you said"

"I know that's good can you call me a cab, I need to stay here out of sight in case they come back"

He had told her that they were not real detectives but criminals who were looking to hurt him. Deena complied, fully taken in by his charm and the fact that he was a good tipper. She didn't care what other people got up to she had to look after herself.

"If they come back tell them what you like, don't get yourself into trouble on my account" He left pressed a fifty note into the receptionist's hand as he said his thank you.

As soon as he saw the detectives were following the man whom Deena had identified Toby walked out of the Hotel and into the waiting taxi.

"Where to sir?" said the cabbie

"Heathrow"

Colin called Jonny. "That's him alright, where are you?"

"About a hundred yards along on the left. He's gone into a local shop"

Colin was already halfway there "Wait with him I'm coming" Colin walked briskly towards where he could see Jonny on the opposite side of the road about to enter the little store. He waited outside having crossed over. The man emerged carrying a newspaper and was opening a bar of chocolate. Jonny was right behind him. "John Smith, I'm a police officer I'd like a word with you"

The man stopped and looked puzzled "I'm sorry I'm not John Smith my name is Winterguard, Barry Winterguard you have the wrong person"

Colin was not sure, the accent was all wrong, northern Newcastle maybe.

"Are you staying at Young's Hotel?"

"Yes, I'm here with the wife we are on holiday here to see the sights of London you know"

"We need to go back to the hotel sir to confirm who you are."

"Ok by me you've got it wrong somehow"

Colin was cursing inside knowing what was coming he had fucked up.

"Is this Mr. Smith he demanded of the receptionist?"

" I don't know. I'll call the police if you cause trouble" she shouted at them.

"What do you mean, we are the police I told you earlier"

"He said you were crooks and were going to break his legs"

"Who did"?

"Mr. Jones"

"Mr. fucking Jones. I don't believe it where is he now?"

"He just left I didn't know I only did what he said" Deena started to cry; her form of defense; she wasn't going to say anymore about Mr. Jones and certainly wasn't going to mention the fifty quid.

He looked at Mr. Winterguard who was smiling at him.

"You sir, can go sorry to have troubled you" Colin was livid with himself taken in by bloody Smith and sodding Jones. If he reported it like it was he would be a laughing stock. Jonny stood to one side saying nothing but thinking the same, he did not relish the idea either. He and Colin would discuss the structure of their report on the way back to Basingstoke. They left Deena with an apology for her distress and assured her no action would be taken for her part in the deception. They fully understood how she had been taken in, it was not her fault.

Right now lets get after that private eye Joseph Mallard, I have an address where his car is registered; it's too not far just south of the river near Wandsworth.

On the way in case they could not find him at this address they both agreed to say that they let the PI go at first in order to apprehend Jones but he was gone from the hotel when we got there. Keep it close to the truth but a lot more simple. No need to mention Smith or Winterguard either. "By the way Mel don't forget to delete Winterguard's photo"

The journey to Wandsworth took almost an hour in traffic. They saw his car parked outside an imposing office block." Not his home this, I hope he is here, park over the road we'll go in together" said Colin.

They saw the name plates at the open doorway. Mallard Investigations on the fift floor. They entered the lift and came to the floor with four offices with different logos. The Mallard name was clear on the closed frosted glass door . They tried the door it opened and as they walked in saw a young girl behind a desk in a small outer office. The door behind her was closed.

" Good afternoon what can I do for you" the girl remained seated.

" I'm Detective Inspector Dale and this is Detective Sergeant Musgrove. We're here to see Joseph Mallard" Colin replied showing her his warrant card.

" I'm sorry he is not in at the moment"

"And you are?"

"I'm Jenny Franks his secretay"

"That's odd his car is down stairs the engines still warm."

"He was here earlier but has gone out again."

" Without his car?"

" I called him a taxi"

"Where was he going"

" I've no idea what's this all about anyway?"

"We just need to ask him a few questions, do you have his mobile number and his home address?"

" I don't think so; you have no right to ask that"

" Oh you don't do you I want to see in his office there just in case you are mistaken"

" It's locked and I don't have a key either please leave now"

"Who is Mr Jones?"

"Never heard of him, you are not welcome here"

Colin pumped her some more but it was obvious she knew nothing of his wherabouts. She was harder than she looked and would not back down with regard to any other information or his address and phone number.

He thought a search of this office would reveal something of who Mallard was working for so knew he would have to get a search warrant before pushing further as registered Private Investigators had some protection with regard their clients data. Evidence obtained without a warrent or information extracted under duress would be useless in court, a big no no with their Chief.

"You can play it like that Miss Franks but we'll be back with our warrant"

On the way back to Hampshire the journey was quiet. They were both thinking not a good result and felt peeved that they had fallen for such a simple ruse. One thing was sure whoever this Mr. Jones really is he will not get away with that type of trick again. He would get that warrant and dig deep into that PI's business.

Joseph had returned to his office briefly. He knew he should go through his files and remove any that related to Toby, but thinking about it there was not much commited to paper or on his office computer so he didn't bother. He grabbed his laptop, passport and his overnight case which he always had ready in his office. There was nothing to go to his home for, he kept the bare minimum of personal items there as he spent most of his life on the move. "Jenny love I have to go away for a few days if any one comes looking stall them for me I don't want to be disturbed"

"Sure thing anything I can do?" She knew not to ask where he was going, what she didn't know she couldn't tell was Joseph's philosophy.

"Yes...yes call me a taxi ta. I'll call you in a few days. I'll wait for the cab downstairs. Close the office tonight and stay at home untill you get my call" With that Joseph pecked her on the cheek and walked out.

Jenny was use to his abrupt ways as he often went away like this however this was a bit sudden maybe a bit of trouble brewing, Joseph had left just in time as the uninvited visitors turned up before Jenny could close up and leave.

Chapter 32

Sandra was desperate; her description was in the evening paper with a photo fit picture as a person of interest in a murder investigation. The accompanying article didn't say much except for anyone who knows her to contact the police. "How the hell did they find out" She thought she was safe.

She did not know what to do she was afraid to go out in case someone saw her. Toby was not answering his mobile, or the number of his London apartment. He must be at one of the houses. She tried ringing them all but no answer. She sent texts and e-mails again no response. She was thinking what could have happened. "Perhaps the police were on to him and had been arrested, not likely he was too clever for that, he must be lying low that's it. He would contact her when he was ready to leave."

She paced the floor of her apartment getting more and more agitated. Her mind was in a turmoil.

"It must have been that Fairbanks bitch she's remembered already. We should have let Gerry go away, his death had opened up a can of worms, it was all Toby's fault and now he was gone"

As soon as that thought came into her mind she realised that is exactly what has happened, he had stashed all the money abroad and followed it as soon as he could. "That bastard has fucked off and left me behind to carry the can. Ungrateful sod, I'll kill him"

She sat down to think what she should do. No thoughts of escape came just of revenge. She'd fix them all; first the girl who had been the cause of all this then the police who were on her track and finally Toby. Yes she'd find him wherever he had gone, she had a good idea where that was. "Bloody miles away by now the shit-head I'll pull his sodding teeth out one by one when I find him."

She prepared two needles and took the small hand gun and a full ammunition clip from her bedside cabinet drawer. She put on her dark clothes, trousers, flat shoes and her coat with the hood. She called a taxi and waited with vengeance in her heart not knowing where she was going to go. Time did nothing to calm her murderous thoughts her resolve was fixed. Her distorted mind then moved to thoughts of self-preservation.

She told the taxi to wait as she was now thinking more clearly. "Don't rush off like this Sandra" she said to herself. If she was being sought by the police the dark clothes were a mistake she needed to change her appearance. She gave the taxi driver a tenner for his trouble and let him go.

She turned back into her flat and immediately went to her wardrobe looking for clothing different to her normal dark attire. She chose jeans and a red sweatshirt with a red scarf and trainers. A clash of colours she would never normally wear. She always wore her long hair up, some times plaited and, as now, often in a bun. She let her hair hang long and brushed it out to give it more volume. She removed her always immaculte make up added just a light powder to whiten her dark complexion. She then changed her lipstic from a strong red to a dull shade almost brown. She was amazed how different she appeared. She tended to carry herself with a slight stoop to disguise her large frame but decided to walk tall from now on. A short light blue puffa jacket completed the new look.

She would go to Joseph Mallard's first he might know where Toby had gone in any case he would probably know a bit more about what was going on with the investigation than she did. She called another taxi and headed first for the private investigator's office.

Sandra saw that Joseph's Honda was parked outside his office in its usual place. "Good he's in" she thought. She told the taxi to wait and walked throught the front door of the multi-occupancy block. Josephs office was on the fifth floor. She waited impatiently for the lift not knowing what she was going to say.

The opaque half glass door with 'Mallard Investigations' painted on in black was closed. She pushed it open and enterred the outer reception area where Joseph's girlfriend come secretary Jenny normally sat. No one was there. She called out with no reply. She moved to the door of the inner office to find it locked. She banged on the door and called out again, still no response. Just then Jenny walked in.

"Oh... Sandra it's you, I didn't recognise you at first you look different, sorry I was just in the loo, Joseph is out at the moment what can I do for you?"

"Where's he gone? His car's outside, will he be long?"

Jenny lied a bit about Joseph's departure this being the second visit of people looking for her man. The police interest was bad enough but they had to follow rules, Sandra was a different ball game, she and her boss Toby were people Jenny feared much more.

"I don't think he will be back today, he left before I got up this morning and wasn't here when I got in, he left a note to say he had been called away for a few days on a new job. It said he would call me at home this evening"

"Have you tried phoning him?"

"Yes of course but his phone is switched off, he took his passport and an overnight bag so may be flying off somewhere abroad. He does that sometimes. He doesn't tell me much about his cases like that."

Sandra was suspicious but although Jenny seemed to be unphased by Joseph's sudden departure the coincidence of both men having disappeared was a real concern for Sandra. " Jenny please tell him to call me the minute you hear from him I have a job I need him to do" She did not expect Joseph would call but did not want to alarm Jenny so that she held out on her if he returned or even worse if he didn't she might contact the police with a missing persons report.

What to do next to protect herself began to play on her mind. She returned to the taxi and headed to her flat. She wished to pack a bag and pick up her passport. She stopped off at an ATM and drew her daily maximum of four hundred pounds from her current account. Her substatial wealth was tied up here in property and shares. She thought that by now she would be living it up on the small fortune that Toby has salted away. Unlike him she did not have offshore accounts to call on so leaving everything she owned behind to avoid arrest was not an easy option. She could draw cash on anther two credit cards that were in her flat. That would give her enough money to lie low for a few days whilst she eliminated the source of her troubles. She did not want to use her cards away from home as they were too easy to trace. Finding Toby would have to wait.

Chapter 33

She was again rising to the thoughts of avoiding identification and vengence. To that end Harriet Fairbanks was to be her target. She looked up suitable accomodation on the net and obtained a phone number where she booked a small B&B near the hospital. She would travel to Basingstoke tonight and stay there where cash was acceptable and anonimity likely. Her new look would help her avoid detection.

A confident Sandra sat on the train her mind playing the scenario of her plan to eliminate Faibanks altogether. The news reports of the accident had said that the girl had been taken to a local hospital, Sandra expected she would still be there she would find out later thinking. "I should have got rid of her in the beginning instead of that stupid elaborate plan made up by that arsehole Toby".

She arrived too late to go to the hospital now, a stranger wandering about asking questions this time of night would draw too much attention, she would have to wait. She deposited her bag in left luggage at the station. With her small handbag only she took the short taxi ride to her digs, which she found was much closer to the hospital than first thought. "Good I can walk there in the morning when everyone will be busy"

She told the landlady that she would only be staying a couple of days and paid her in advance, explaining that she was visiting a sick friend and may leave from the hospital directly without coming back.

The morning could not have come too soon, Sandra was awake well before dawn her mind going back to when life was less complex and Toby was her soulmate. She rose, dressed and went down to be greeted by the offer of a 'Full English' which she declined requesting some coffee and toast.

She was offered a local paper which she accepted and scanned for any report that might be relevant, but nothing jumped out as important.

At nine thirty Sandra walked through the front doors of the hospital. She knew that trying to find her target by wandering around the wards would be near impossible so approached the front desk to make her enquirey. The porter on duty had a log of all patients and their location. She asked politely of the whereabouts of Harriet. She watched his face for signs of alarm as he scanned the screen. No tell tales there, as he guided her to Ward C3 Medical. "It's a bit early love visiting's not till this afternoon"

Luckily for Sandra although the police had put a watch on Harriet ward they had neglected to inform the front desk to flag up relevant requests for information.

Sandra purchased a bunch of flowers at the hospital shop to cement her role as a visitor and walked towards the lifts that would take her to floor C. On exiting the lift she made a note of the location of the staircase which she would use on her way out.

She looked for the signs for ward 2 and followed the wide corridor to be confronted by a pair of swing doors with glass window in the top. Wanting to get the layout in her head without fear of dicovery she assumed the layout of ward 2 would be similar to ward 3 her true target. She looked through but could see nothing that would guide her to her to who occupied which. She braved the doors pushing them open with her knees walked through looking left and right into what were private single occupancy rooms. Some were occupied others were empty. At the end of this hallway was a nurses station two staff were sitting behind the counter, she could see that the ward extended to the left and right with units of six or so beds in each. She walked passed the station as if she were quite used to doing this.

"Excuse me miss can I help you?" The nurse nearest had stood up from behind the counter "I'm sorry visiting time is not untill later"

" Oh dear I didn't know I've come down from London to visit my friend Joan Grey."

"Visiting is not untill two this afternoon"

"That's a pity can I say hello and leave her these flowers at least?"

"I don't see why not however I don't think your friend is on this ward, I'll check"

She went to a large white marker board with the names of all the patients, the room and bed numbers and the name of the doctor attending.

"Sorry she is not here you can check at reception they have a record of everyone"

" I already did they told me ward C3"

"Ah...there you go, this is ward C2 you need to go out and turn right along the corridor it is the next ward along"

" Oh my I'm sorry I have been a trouble, thank you"

" That's ok I hope your friend is getting better"

Sandra nodded and left.

Sandra approached C3 with the same air of submissive ignorance. The layout was a mirror image of ward 2. She casually walked up to the nurses station looking in the single rooms as before but did not see he quarry. She approached a nurse sitting at her dek to explain her long trip from London to see her friend Joan Grey and although she understood visiting was not till later asked if she could leave the flowers and say a quick hello.

This nurse was much less friendly " I don't think she is here on this ward" she turned and looked at the whiteboard similar to the one next door. "Sorry no not here"

Sandra appologised and said she would find out where her friend was from the reception and left.

Sanda had seen that Harriet Faibanks name was there on the board as occupying a single room number 4. Puzzled she had passed an empty room 4 in the hallway on the way in, no one was there on the way out either. Sandra thought "She's probably having some treatment or a bath or something I'll come back later during visiting times less conspicuous" Her being in one of the side rooms was a real bonus she could be in and out and no one will notice.

Harriet was not having treatment but was sitting in the visitor room with DC Andrews and Jane Thornby. Their interest in this case had brought them together on a couple of occasions. Peter had been assigned along with two other officers to keep protective watch on Harriet as Toni wanted to be sure her prime witness was kept safe. Jane was just interested in understanding the anomolies of the accident. Having learned of this from Peter she had continued to visit Harriet, partly her natural empathy to see her recover but also as an excuse to spend some time with Peter.

Peter was aware that the afternoon visiting was a danger time. They had arranged the duty changeover with this in mind. It meant two officers were present as several unknown people arrived on the ward. The suspect's description and picture was poor, so close scrutiny would be easier with two pairs of eyes.

Today they were just chatting trying to be a comfort to Harriet. They were well aware of what had happened and the difficulties Harriet faced in coming to terms with her experience.

" I must go now" said Jane "I'll come by tomorrow Harriet if that's ok?"

"Yes it's good to have a visitor who's not a policeman."

Peter let out a mock cry of dismay "Ok you two ganging up on me eh"

"No not really, I would like some of my friends to be able to visit though, I feel so much better now and the doctors say I will be clear of the drugs soon, well almost. Will you ask for me constable if I can?"

" I'll ask but I think DI Webb will not bend yet, she just wants to keep you safe, as do I"

"I know..I know I'll have to be here a little longer so Jane please come when you can that will be great."

"Bye Harriet....Peter I'll see you later"

"Bye" Peter waved as she left the room.

" I'm going back to my room alright"

"Sure I'll stay here for now I'll check on you in a while." Harriet left the room Peter sat quietly thinking about Jane. He liked her well enough but should he ask her out, maybe tomorrow.

Harriet dozed till lunch and found Peter sitting at her bedside when she awoke. She slept a lot partly from boredom but also she was not fully recovered. Another half hour and it would be visiting time the change over due just before. Peter got up after they delivered Harriet's meal and went to the entrance of the ward to meet PC Keith Crane who was the next duty officer. Crane arrived out of uniform as agreed a few minutes early they shook hands. "All quiet as usual I see?"

"Of course, soon be visiting " said Peter "you wait out here and check for anyone who might be our problem, we'll keep the phones open. I'll watch from the girl's room till all the visitors have been checked."

Sandra joined the group of visitors who were waiting for the lift. Clutching a new bunch of flowers and a newspaper she entered then left the lift on floor C along with three others. It was a bit early so she held back untill more people arrived on her floor. Soon there were a dozen or so bodies in the corridor huddled around each of the ward doorways waiting for them to be opened. She held back a little longer looking for anyone who might be more than just a visitor. She waited outside ward 2 looking along the corridor towards ward 3. She spotted PC Crane paying too much attention to the group rather than anticipating the soon to be opened doors . Was he security or was she being paranoid. "Be careful" she thought "Let them go in first before you move." All the visitors bunched together as the doors opened soon to disapear excpet the 'watcher' he used his mobile briefly looking along the corridor in both directions. Sandra stayed close to the ward 2 visitors as they piled in hidden from the 'watcher'. She saw him move into the ward. Sandra waited a full minute before moving from the entrance of ward 2 along the corridor towards ward 3. As she reached the door a young man pushed through with a phone to his ear. She was upon him in a second.

"Is this ward 3?" she asked with her broadest of smiles.

“Yes” he replied without breaking his concentration on his phone..

Thanks” as she passed through the doors into the hallway just a few yards from her quarry.

Peter had the ‘all clear’ from Keith, said good bye to Harriet and left passing Keith Crane who was heading for the nurses station to check in.

“See you tomorrow Peter”

“Fine Keith take care”

Peter decided to call DI Webb for an update, just as the call connected he passed a woman visitor coming in who asked if this was ward 3, he responded positively but concentrating on his phone call. He stopped suddenly feeling oddly chilled, “This is not right she’s abnormally tall, like the description and why ask if ward 3 when it was clearly marked above the door, misdirection?”

He cut the call, spun round and re-entered the ward at speed. The woman was well into Harriets room, he saw that Keith Crane was still down the far end of the hall at the nurse station. Harriet was unprotected he sprinted for the door of room 4 barged it open to see the woman hovering over the sleeping girl a needle poised ready to plunge into her exposed neck. Peter launched himself at her catching her in the small of her back with his shoulder. They both fell back to the floor; as the needle flashed towards him he felt a sharp stab as the point dug into his lower leg. Sandra was forced to let go the syringe before she could press the plunger home. Harriet now awake was screaming as she tumbled out of bed on the opposite side.

They were now both scrambling to get to their feet. They both fell backwards with Sandra on top that gave her a slight advantage as she was the first to rise. Her hand searched her pocket for the second needle but instead it closed around the handle of her pistol. She pulled it out and pointed it at the half risen Peter and fired. The thunderous noise reverberated around the small room. Peter slumped forward clutching his groin. By now Keith had dashed the twenty yards towards room 4 he arrived just as Sandra was leaving, she raised her pistol again but was too slow as he head butted her in the stomach smashing her into the wall. She raised the gun again but used it as a club striking Keith on the top of his head with such force that it jerked from her hand as he fell to his knees unconcious.

Both protectors out of it Sandra made the fateful decision to go after Harriet so turned back this time her hand found the second needle as she stepped into the room. Harriet was waiting and launched her body at her attacker grabbing the arm holding the deadly spike. The attempted stab from Sandra missed and as Harriet twisted her arm away and up, the point dug deep into Sandra's face right through the flesh of her cheek. She screamed and as they fell the plunger hit the floor ejecting its deadly contents into Sandra's mouth. She tried not to swallow attempting to spit out the vile fluid; she coughed and spluttered but much of the poison was already working it's way down her gullet. She lifted herself clear of Harriet kicked her weakly in the side and stumbled from the room yanking the needle from her cheek. She ran along the long corridor her mind intent on escape, her fingers were pushing down her throat as she moved trying to be sick. All she did was retch but nothing came up. She came upon the planned stairwell went through the door to her escape.

Harriet crawled over to Peter praying he was still alive. He was semi-concious holding his groin and moaning. Within minutes Mike Smith had arrived and was stemming the flow of blood from the wound in the top of Peters leg where the bullet had entered. The orderlies moved him immediately to the operating theatre where he was soon under the knife of the duty surgeon. Keith had recovered concousness by then and was being tended by the nurses he had been chatting to a short time earlier.

Sandra ran and ran down the road towards the town centre and the railway station, she could feel the drugs begint to fog her mind but her resolve was strong. She knew she must not stop, she must keep moving or she would succumb to the powerful narcotic. She cut through the council estate running all the way oblivious to the stares of the people she passed. She was sure she had swallowed only part of the drug if she could only get to the station she could get a drink and dilute the contents of her stomach, maybe some salt water where she could force herself to be sick. The station was in sight, she struggled up the stairs to the platform with the café.

It was closed “shit..shit” she shouted out loud. She stumbled to a platform bench her breath coming in short gasps and almost collapsed onto it. He mind was racing with what to do, she knew she must keep awake and breathe deeply. The mist slowly engulfed her vision and her mind’s eye drifted away and down looking on darkness. A long sleep was upon her, a very very long sleep.

Chapter 34

They found Sandra's body sitting on a bench on the same platform where she had first encountered Gerry. It was amazing that she had made it that far, although instantly fatal when injected the drugs took much longer, when ingested, to have the same but inevitable effect.

Once she had been identified Colin and Toni and a full forensic team went to London, searched her flat and her old office at W.W. Enterprise. Forensic evidence linking her to Gerry Grey was found at the appartment. There was almost a small lab in one of the bathrooms where the drugs she concockted were assembled along with various syringes.

Her office revealed the many dealings that she and Toby had been involved in. Her diary was the most revealing baring open her twisted psychopathic mind. It would need careful analysing to separate the truth from her demented ramblings but may prove useful in tracking down her mentor David Charles known as Toby Cutler-Jones.

They had traced his departure from London, under his real name to Madrid, but after that the trail was stone cold. A change in appearance a new name and passport he could have gone anywhere. A difficult search for someone that's for sure.

Craig Bean stood in the hushed squadroom. Everyone at the station was sqeezed into that one space.

"Thanks for leaving your current tasks to be here but I think it is important that I put you in the picture with what has happened recently. We have been incredibly lucky today not to have lost one if not two of our officers not to mention a key witness. The incident however ended in the death of our prime suspect. I can assure you that this death was not, I repeat not, caused by the action of our officers. There will however be an external enquiry where some if not all of you will be interviewed. Please be open and cooperate fully. In the mean time do not discuss this with anyone even your colleages, I don't want rumors starting from here and I certainly don't want the press to have anything other than official statements for their sources of information.

Moving on Detective Constable Peter Andrews is now out of surgery. They have removed a bullet from his pelvis which had entered through his leg.

I'm told he will make a full recovery. He is very lucky, if you can say being shot is lucky, that he was not killed. Constable Keith Crane is also ok, he will have a huge bump and a sore head but no permanent damage, he will be kept in for a day or two for observation."

"Head like a rock that one" someone piped up from the back of the room. There was a ripple of laughter that helped to lighten the sombre mood.

Craig continued "Good job too it could have been much worse. Moving on, our witness Harriet Fairbanks was unhurt thanks to the action of these brave officers. DI Webb here will now brief the investigation team on their next tasks, the rest of you can go, thank you gentlemen and ladies. Over to you Toni."

"Thank you sir; right then..." Toni paused to let the room empty to where only her officers and those who normally worked there were left. " Our suspect's body is now in autopsy, dead we suspect from an accidental poisoning, we'll wait for the results before rather than speculate further. There are too many loose ends to prove definitely that our suspect is the murderer. Her name is Sandra Cooper but as sure as I am that she killed Gerry Grey I'm also certain that she was not the only one involved. We need to question the private investigator Joseph Mallard. It would be good to trace the anonymous tip that threw up her name. The jackers that left prints have yet to be found. I leave that to you and your team DI Dale?"

"That's fine, I will need to be based in London for a while to get somewhere with that?"

"I'm sure DCI Craig will approve the expence and overtime, but leave Constable Frazer to help Compton Busion they have done well working together so far."

It seems likely that this David Jones may be central as he has gone abroad with a very large sum of money. That must definitley be followed up which will be for me and Sergeant Mann.

Harriet was onto something with this Jones character and his company W.W. Enterprises. We have retrieved lots of electronic data from Sandras files found in the her old office. That's a job for you Constable Busion. Harriet is ready and willing to work with you on finding out why she was their target. She must have hit a nerve there somewhere.

She is still far from recovery so don't expect too much, there are large gaps in her memory and many that she does remember are false induced by the drugs.

We are waiting for the autopsy of Sandra Cooper but are sure her death was due to the poison she swallowed from her own syringe. Her DNA may conclusivley tie her to Gerry and him to her boss David Jones.

We know there was a major sell off of W.W. Entreprises with most of the money gone with Jones overseas. It seems well above board but knowing what has gone on I have my doubts. If we dig a little we may unearth a bag real unsavoury worms.

Chapter 35

Peter, who had slept several hours after being moved from recovery to a side ward, awoke not knowing where he was. His vision was blurred so tried to lift his hand to wipe away the sleep from his eyes but found it being held.

Jane had been with him since then. “Hello there sleepy head, thought you’d never wake” Jane squeezed his hand gently as his eyes tried to focus. He rubbed them with his free hand recognising his new friend and understood where he was.

“Jane….what….?

“ Take it easy there you are going to be fine”

Memories of what had happened came flooding back, his mind jumped into overdrive full of questions.”What happened to Harriet is she all right, did Crane get her is he ok, did she get away?”

“Hey hey wait a moment one question at a time please, no one was hurt except you”

“She shot me…she shot me..I thought I was dead I thought she wouuld kill Harriet”

“Relax…relax everything is ok Harriet is fine Constable Crane has a lump on his head you are the only one who matters that got hurt. The woman who did all this is dead."

"Wow....who...how.... that's a relief... we should have spotted her sooner... she almost got to Harriet it was my fault she could have been killed"

" You and Keith did your jobs, she is alive thanks to you; mind you she did her share and gave that woman a big surprise too"

"You said she was dead....did Harriet...do..."

"Oh no no the woman fell on the syringe during her struggle to get away and died later, serves her right if you ask me"

"Peter went to move to be greeted with a sharp and stabbing pain in his lower back.

"Ooooh...shit that hurts"

"Not surprising it isn't everyday you get shot in the arse, I'll ask the nurse for some pain killers; by the way your Mum and Dad are here. They've been with you most of the night, I sent them off for a cuppa they were dead on their feet, they'll be back in a minute"

Jane left to go to the nurses station to organise some pain medication. Peter again attempted to sit up he manage to move a bit but the pain stopped him from sitting up fully. He pulled down his covers to have a look at his wound. His upper leg was all wrapped in bandages right up to the middle of his back he wondered what they'd done to him.

"What do you mean shot in the arse?" he demanded when Jane returned.

" My little joke really, you were shot in the leg but as you were almost horizontal the bullet travelled up the leg and lodged in your pelvic bone quite close to your 'arse' ok. They removed the bullet and stitched you up here and there. It missed your femoral artery, that would have been much more serious, so you're going to be sore for a while but fine in a few weeks."

Mum and Dad then walked into his room with Mum near to tears when she saw him awake. Then began the inquisition. Jane said her goodbyes with the promise to return later, leaving Peter happy to be alive but straining to answer his Mum's multitude of questions. A short relief from motherly fussing came in the form of a nurse bearing his pain medicine.

Chapter 36

Craig was not a happy man, he knew he should have done more, become more involved.

Two officers hurt and a suspect dead not a good conclusion in fact not a conclusion at all there were too many unanswered questions.

He had let his two Detective Inspectors run the show with the minimum of interference. He wanted Toni Webb to show that his choice was the right one, in doing so he had put Colin Dale on the defensive and instead of working in harmony they had been operating separately. Toni had tried her best to smooth the situation but had not had time to establish herself with her new colleagues before being thrust into this case. His lack of hands on had led to things being missed, it seemed like the Jones character had inside information as he was one step ahead all the time and had left this crazy woman Sandra Cooper to bear the consequences.

He was sitting in his office with the two DIs sitting opposite an uncomfortable silence hung there with the unexpressed thoughts of the three.

"Colin Toni where do you go from here? Let me have your ideas"

Toni opened "The autopsy of Sandra Cooper showed that she died of the same cocktail as Gerry Grey. His DNA was found on her body in several places and her's on him. It would seem that she had killed her lover, we don't know why for certain..."

Colin interrupted " It would be my guess that she coaxed him to stage the accident of Harriet Fairbanks, whether he was party to the torture inflicted by Cooper we don't know, but once Harriet was out of the way he was no longer needed so she disposed of him. The drugs and the means used on both were found in her flat. We now have CCTV footage from Shoreditch that puts them together and her at Basingstoke station on two occasions with one just a short time after the killing. We would have had a solid case against her I'm sure"

" That's all well and good, but we don't know why Harriet was the target, are we any nearer an answer to that one?"

" Look we can draw a line under the Gerry Cooper case, can't we?" Toni looked at Craig who did not answer her rhetorical question. " What we must do now is to follow up with tracing Jones and anyone associated, I am of a mind that he is behind all this. PC Busion has established a link between Jones and the private investigator Joseph Mallard both have now gone missing. Jones for certain had control over Cooper for sure"

Colin cut in "Look we can only follow up with what we've got, I have just obtained a search warrant for his office so am sure I can track down Joseph Mallard and maybe get some information about his relatioship with Jones, he won't have gone far or for long he has too much here to lose. He'll have some explaining to do when I catch up with him."

"Ok Colin I leave that to you and your team. Toni can you get a full backgound check on Jones and see if we can find out where he has gone. Oh and get Compton to continue with her investigation into his business dealings particularly this recent sale. I know you are without Andrews but PCs June Owens and Keith Crane can help you for now, it may be some time before Andrews is fit."

"Thank you sir, Peter and I were just starting to work together early days for us, I like him, he'll be back. The other officers will be fine for now; we have a lot to do if we are to clear up all these loose ends."

They all stood, almost together "I'll close the Grey murder case leave all the paperwork to me just make your files available, you have enough on your hands for now with all that"

Craig sat down as the others left pleased that things were moving again, he didn't know where to but trusted his DIs to get some results. He had taken on the thankless task of closing the murder case as an appeasement to his own concience.

Within a few minutes Craig was looking through the case files when Fred Mann came knocking on his door, he waved him in.

"What can I do for you sergeant?"

Fred poked his head round the door. "Can I have a word sir?"

"Please come in and sit down Fred, is something wrong?"

"Sorry sir I know this is not a good time what with Peter in hospital and the new DI and all but I've had enough. This job and looking after Fiona it's too much and I'm not doing either properly. I've been to see young Andrews thank God he was not killed I should have been there. What it boils down to is that I'm not much use to you any more so I would like to go for my pension."

"You know Fred I'm not surprised it's been coming a while now. As for your being no use that's just rubbish.We'll miss you more than you think you'll leave a big gap, very hard to fill. The others will just have to manage but don't you fret about that"

Fred didn't respond he seemed miles away Craig was concerned that the past few weeks had taken a serious toll on his old colleague's well-being.

"You still have some leave this year don't you? Hand over your stuff to PC Owens get away from here for a few days whilst I sort this pension stuff out for you. I'll need a letter of resignation with a request for retirement for the Personnel Department. Don't worry leave all that to me when it's done I'll give you a call, all you'll have to do is sign and you will be a free man. Personnel will contact you with a date and a figure for your pension, now you go home to Fiona"

"Thanks Craig you've been a big help to me over Fi's illness; I've let you and Peter down I know but...."

"But nothing Fred, you cannot be held responsible for that maniac's actions. We've known each other a long time as colleagues and friends, go along with you now take it easy and relax you've earned it"

Fred raised a false smile, he was feeling far from relaxed. A free man indeed; no chance. Now he needed to leave before it all came crashing down. He had seen the photos of the private investigator taken by Colin and Jonny on the stakeout at Harriets flat. It was the same guy that had given him Toby's money on Esher station. What if they catch him and bring him here it would be all over if he saw me. No doubt he'd give Fred up in a second to save his skin. His hope was that Toby had been his usual secretive self. He may have not let on who Fred really was so was not known by Joseph Mallard only by sight.

"Thanks sir...err...Craig, I'll be going then. Is it all right if I call in now and again to see how the case is going, it would be nice to leave knowing it was all cleared up."

" Of course... of course you can. Well goodbye for now Fred I'll see you soon take care."

Fred Mann left the office and went in search of June Owens, he wanted to brief her and be gone as soon as he could. He didn't want Colin suddenly popping up in Basingstoke with the PI in tow. There was fear in his heart that his past was about to catch him at the last hurdle he was hoping 'out of sight out of mind.'

Joseph was sure he was being followed and this business with Tony was certainly not as straight as it appeared. Sandra was a crazy bitch all sweetness when she wanted something but a devil with a twisted mind when crossed. She doted on Toby but could turn in a second. He wanted to be well away and let things cool down before surfacing again. He had taken the cash he always kept in reserve told Jenny to keep quiet and act the innocent. She was good at that, lots of practice with clients looking for him. He took a cab to Victoria Station, then underground to Paddington for a train to the West country this being his choice for a quiet month or two, he would not be found easily.

Chapter 37

A whole week had gone by, Toni was feeling depressed they were no nearer to finding Jones or Mallard. Her and Colin had followed every avenue only to meet a dead end each time. The two men had covered their tracks well. Although they had established a link to Jones from files that were found in the PI's office they had little useful information mostly invoices and expence receipts for surveillance unspecified. They knew from airline data and passport control that Jones had gone to Africa through Europe but after that the trail went cold. They tried to follow the money but it had been transferred several times to accounts in Switzerland, the Caymen Islands and South America but the trail had gone cold thereafter. The money in Africa, more than a million dollars, had been used to buy diamonds, this had been done legitimately, it was his money after all.That was the easiest way to carry cash in great quantities and Toby had used that method before to move money without trace. It seemed like he was laughing at them.

Investigations into his former business and the sale of W.W. Enterprises to the consortium had revealed nothing unusual, the Consortium investors were sure they had achieved a very good deal, not only had they acquired an excellent portfolio of office and residential buildings in London providing continuous cash flow from rents, the new development would yield a very high return once completed.

Constable Busion was not convinced that all was right concerning the transaction, Toby Jones was not the type to sell cheap and walk away from a big profit, there must have been something wrong with that deal; something that Harriet had stumbled onto that required her to be silenced for a while. Why the torture though, did they want information? That was only really known by Sandra, it seems that maybe she just enjoyed it, the thought made Compton shudder. She had interviewed Harriet about her invetigation into W.W. and Toby's business, had gone through her files only coming up with his large and unusual money transfers. There was no real evidence of any wrong doings there.

Harriette's investigation into the sale of W.W. Enterprises to the Consortium had only just started. Toby had been quick to buy the land with little delay from it becoming available to it being in the hands of W.W. Unusual in itself as Toby was usually more meticulous than that. Normally he would look for big profits to be made but would investigate thoroughly to be sure there was little risk before commiting himself to a contract. This was different he had been greedy to grow his company as fast as he could; then why not see it to a conclusion? If he had stayed to complete the project it would have put him amongst the 'Big Boys' which had been his burning ambition all along, so why off-load it?

It suddenly struck Compton Busion, that was it! He had indeed 'off-loaded it' It had become a problem. The land acquisition had made W.W. a liability. She needed to research the history of the land, Toby had discovered a flaw in his plans and wanted rid before nosey Harriet found out and scuppered his plans to sell off the company.

She would go to the boss with this as she needed to go to London and dig out some files from land registry, very old ones that had never been put on computer databases. She was getting closer to an answer she could feel the warm glow of excitement rising, this was her reason for being here.

Craig called Toni into his office, “Compton here has come up with something I think needs looking into.” The PC outlined her theory Toni immediately came to the same conclusion “This could be the motive we have been missing since day one.” She looked at her watch. “Lets go if we hurry we should get to the land registry office before they close”

Craig smiled to himself as they both left, it’s coming together at last, thinking ‘even if we don’t catch up with this Jones character we can at least put out an international warrant for his arrest. All we need now is for Colin Dale to catch up with the PI Joseph Mallard and we could close this case.’

He settled back in his chair and looked at the mound of paperwork remembering fondly the days long gone when he was out doing police work not tied to a desk. His first task was to process Fred Mann’s retirement. ‘My turn next probably, the way is now opening for the likes of an ambitious Toni Webb and young graduates like Peter Andrews.’

Chapter 38

The end came sooner than anyone thought with orders from above the following day. A.C.C. Moore had closed the case even though Jones and Mallard had not been found. There was no direct evidence that either had contributed to the abduction of Harriet or the murder of Gerry Grey, although the theory that Jones had wanted Harriet silenced had been agreed as most likely, there was no proof.

Sandra Cooper was the one who had abducted Harriet and had also murdered Gerry Grey. Her motives could have been to follow her boss's instructions it could just as likely have been her psychopathic desire to inflict pain.

The Assitant Chief Constable had come to Craig's office to deliver the news personally. "I'm sorry Craig but the Chief Constable is adamant we must stop wasting money and resources chasing persons whom we have insufficient evidence to prosecute. Jones has gone away with his own legitimate money as has Joseph Mallard. You have nothing to arrest them for. Close the case now and put your teams to work on dealing with things closer to home." He rose and left DCI Bean with no alternative. Craig was glad in some ways, he would like to go back to the days of dealing with the low level crime which was more common on his patch. In his heart he regretted that the lack of funds determined justice or in this case the lack of it. He would call everyone in tomorrow and shut this thing down.

"Good morning team" Craig looked round the room to see that he had his officers attention. "I have some mixed news this morning, the good news is that the investigation into the murder of Gerry Grey by Sandra Cooper is now officially closed." There was a universal murmer of accent and an almost joint sigh of relief from one and all."

The not so good news is that we are to wind up the current investigation into David Jones and Joseph Mallard." This time the noise was a universal groan with several negative expletives. Toni jumped to her feet "Why on earth are we shutting down when we are so near. We are close to finding his motive yesterday at the records office, the land that Jones bought has no records. The security there is appalling, the files were taken out for study in one of their public reading rooms several weeks ago we think by Jones or Mallard; the contents were removed and replaced with blank paper before being returned to the issuing clerk. He just took the file at face value before putting it back into the storage facility. None of these old files have been commited to digital or microfisch copy. We are checking the prints found on the file covers and the paper as we speak. We are sure there is a problem with the land that will now link Jones and maybe Mallard directly to the abduction of Harriet Fairbanks, she needed to be kept quiet until the sale of his company was completed. Please boss we are nearly there we must continue with this."

"I understand your frustration matching prints to Jones means nothing, he would have investigated the files as part of his purchase he could have found them blank just as you have, you still don't have definitive proof. Regardless of where we all think we are the order has come from the Chief Constable so we will stop all further work on this as from now. To continue this we would be outside our area and treading on the London police toes, they have been tollerant up to now but us investigating a London based Company will not be acceptable. Their fraud squad will be looking at that . We are to send all our information to the Met. who will investigate the source of the stolen vehicles as well. Now that the murder and abduction cases have been closed we don't have the time, funds or authority to proceed further" More moans and groans came from the assembly.

DI Colin Dale stepped in "I think if we continued we could get a good result here. I have not found Joseph Mallard yet, we know from CCTV that he has gone to the West country by train. It is only a matter of time before we catch up with him, he could be the key to finding Toby Jones however catching up with him and forcing him to leave is a very different matter. Even if we had a watertight case for the C.P.S. we can't bring him to justice easily as we don't even know which continent he is on let alone which country."

Craig continued "I know we are all upset that we cannot conclude this to our satisfaction, the resources are just not there and that's the bottom line. There you have it, write up your reports now and add any new data you may have to the files, please complete this by the close of play today." Craig left the squadroom still buzzing with the murmers of discent.

'Bloody funding always buggers things up' he was thinking as he walked slowly back to his office.

Toni looked at Compton " That was a waste of a trip, so near yet so far"

"We could have had him Ma'am, I wonder what was in those files"

" We may never find out Constable, but you never know what may turn up either" Toni was thinking she would not let this go she would quietly keep her sights on Toby Cutler-Jones.

Toni accepted that the official line would be followed but she would still continue with an under the counter investigation. First establish whose prints were on those land registry files. She would speak to Colin Dale to see where they were with finding Joseph Mallard and ask him to keep pushing. A lot could be done without upsetting the politics from above. This man Jones had caused a death, a torture a shot colleage and probably a major fraud. She couldn't abide the thought that he was sitting on a sunny beach somewhere laughing at their futile efforts to tie him down. She would not let this one go so easily. She had an idea that Colin Dale would be of the same mind. Let the dust settle a while and see if the London guys are really interested in the case or are just playing politics. She had plenty of contacts there who will keep her in the picture and a few owed favours she could call on if necessary.

Chapter 39

Peter was given the news in hospital by Toni concerning the case. He expressed his sorrow that all their work had come to nothing but felt glad that he could return to normal police functions and that he would probably not have to face that dangerous situation again. He was surprised that Sergeant Mann was gone and he made a resolution to visit him as soon as he was well enough.

"Do you know when you are coming out?"

"They said I will have some physio tomorrow when they will assess my mobility. If I can walk with crutches the'll let me home. I will go to Mum and Dad's place for a while it will be better than the police house. I've no idea when I will be back at work but as soon as I can I'll be there. I hope we can continue to work together or will you find another DC?"

"You take your time young man, your job with me will be there no matter how long, don't rush it coming back too soon will be a mistake. You must take some councelling too, I will arrange that, they can visit you at your parent's home or you can come to them whatever you want."

"I'm all right you know, in my mind that is, I don't need that, the leg hurts a bit but I feel ok in myself"

"You have no choice, it is a police procedure that has to be done, when you have suffered trauma you may feel fine now but it may come back to haunt you when put in danger again. We need to make sure there will be no problems for you in the future. It doesn't have to be for long, if you are really ok they will sign you off pretty quick, they are good at their job these therapists."

"OK I accept that it has to be done, I would prefer to go to them I don't want my Mum and Dad worried by this any more that necessary"

"OK I'll let you know where to go, you'll get a letter explaining who when and where.

I still have to find a new sergeant as Fred has finally gone, strange that right in the middle of the case too. PCs Busion and Crane will back me up for now."

" Hope Crane is ok, does he have to have therapy too?"

"He's fine back at work straight away. I'm not sure a bump on the head is classed as trauma, not like getting shot, although he was at just as much risk as you so maybe, not my decision that will be up to the chief. I'll be going now, I'll look in on you again soon that's if they don't let you out before. Goodbye Peter " A quick wave of the hand as Toni Webb left the bedside and headed for the station.

Peter was itching to get out of the hospital and into the care of his Mum, she'd feed him up and fuss him to death which will help him well on the road to recovery and with those thoughts of home comforts he drifted off to sleep.

Jane was sitting beside him reading a magazine when he woke. "There you are" she said "Sleeping again"

"Oh...hello what a nice surprise, how long have you been there?"

She stood, leaned over and pecked him on the cheek "Not long, you look much better today a bit more colour"

" I do feel more myself thanks. I've just had a visit fom the DI, she said I had to have some sort of therapy, it's police rules when you've been shot or some such thing. I'm going to my parents from here until I can cope on my own, didn't fancy the staff house by myself"

"That's a pity I was looking forward to looking after you a bit"

Peter felt embarrassed at sudden thoughts of being mothered by Jane. " Well I won't be away any longer than I need maybe just a week or two, you could come and visit if you like on your days off, you can stay over if you want there's plenty of room"

It was Jane's turn to feel odd, where was this going? The conversation had taken a very personal turn one that she rather liked. "I'd enjoy that" she responded." Let me know where it is and I will look up my free days"

"How's work?"

"Not too busy the usual knocks and sick older people who neglect themselves, no real dramas. I'm on duty a bit later so can stay for half an hour or so"

Their conversation continued for some time with the trivia of the day and of each other plans for the future until it was time for Jane to leave.

Chapter 40

Fred had his first good nights sleep for months. The announcement that the murder case was to be closed and that the search for Toby and Joseph had been called off was music to his ears. He had kept abreast of what was happening through young Constable Busion thank goodness for limited budgets, it seemed now they had come to his rescue was it possible that he was home and dry?

His pension had come through quite a bit more than he thought as the extra years had been adding to his pot without him realising. They had enough for Fred to have some help and the new stairlift was on its way. He felt guilty about the source of the money but it did reveal the name of Sandra Cooper which helped to conclude that terrible episode. Some small consolation when it could have been a disaster. All he wanted was peace and now he may have some at last.

Chapter 41

Toby Jones had travelled to Brazil through four countries using a different passport on each leg of the journey. Currently known as Alan Mortimer his chosen new identity and backgound being as solid as one could buy, with a genuine passport and life history that would hold up under the closest of scrutiny. He was sitting in the living room of the house he had rented on a small island in the resort of Busios. The climate here was unique, it stayed warm all year but being on the shore the breeze made it very pleasant even on the hottest days. His house keeper/cook only spoke Potugese as did his gardener come poolman. He was happy with that as he managed to communicat fine with a few newly learnt words and sign language; a bonus being she was an exceptional cook. He was very comfortable and could stay here a long time and would do so if necessary.

Busios was a group of five islands in Brasil, four hundred miles north of Rio de Janero linked to the mainland by a causeway and some bridges. The mainland entrance was guarded by the local police so no one came in who was not supposed to be there. Many of the homes were weekender's pads whos owners usually arrived by helicopter from Rio. There were bars and restaurants nightclubs and the ever warm sea. There were places to shop where you could buy anything you wanted, a real closed community where everyone smiled and no one asked any questions. 'Alan' was going to enjoy it here. He had plenty of time to plan his return to Britain, there was no rush. He felt safe here with paid protection insulating him from any external interference. He had plenty of American dollars in a local bank and his diamonds were in his safe deposit at American Express office in Rio. What more could a man need. He needed to be busy, wheeling and dealing was his lifeblood, he may get involved in something here whilst his plans to return home evolved. For now was the close of the first part of his life. This was the birth place of his new beginning.

Epilogue

Newspaper Report DAILY MAIL Finance Page

'It was announced today that CITY DEVELOPMENT CORPORATION PLC would not be seeking planning consent to develop the land acquired as part of their buy-out of WW Enterprises eight months previous. A spokesman said the site was not suitable for the originally proposed housing project and would be looking for alternative uses. Once mixed farmland the site has remained unused for several decades. It was thought that the council encouraged and indeed welcomed this development but the spokesman declined to state the reasons for this decision. Their shares dropped sharply by sixty five pence to two zero six following the announcement. The shares recovered slightly to two one one by close of todays market'

Newspaper Report BASINGSTOKE GAZETTE

Basingstoke Police Station announced the retirment of two of its long standing officers. Detective Chief In spector Craig Bean and Sergeant Fredrick Mann. Both local men, they have been working for Hampshire Police for many years. Craig said "I have been a policeman for most of my life and it has been an honour to have served this community but I have now reached a time where the younger men will continue the work in a more modern and technically based force" Fred left some months earlier to look after his sick wife. Detective Inspector Toni Webb has been promoted to the post of Chief Inspector following the retirement. Mrs. Webb is the first female Chief Inspector at Basingstoke. Born in Nigeria but living in England since a small child she was transferred from Southampton seven months ago. *DI Colin Dale was also promoted to DCI and transferred back to his former station in London. We wish them well in their retirement and in their new positions.'*

Printed in Poland
by Amazon Fulfillment
Poland Sp. z o.o., Wrocław